THE GREEN GRASS TANGO

BERYL GILROY

THE GREEN GRASS TANGO

PEEPAL TREE

First published in Great Britain in 2001
Peepal Tree Press Ltd
17 King's Avenue
Leeds LS6 1QS
England

ISBN 1 900715 47 3

FOREWORD

This is a story about people in a London park, some of whom had been turned out of their shelters, refuges, mental hospitals, council flats during the Thatcher years. Why did not concern anyone; they were simply turned out to live in 'the community', something that did not exist because of the transience of populations and the fact that people in London do not, in general, fraternise with their next-door neighbours.

Nevertheless here were people in the park, on the pavement or in any makeshift shelter being at one with their friends, establishing a community of sorts. Because of their frequent isolation, when they talked they 'streamed' their consciousness, and indeed their unconscious, in a free flowing way. Talk turned to dogs, cats, pigeons – those creatures with which they frequently shared their food in love and generosity.

Widowed, I got myself a most intelligent dog for company, and found myself in the park each morning. In time, because of my dog, I was admitted to the group – smart, respectable, dead-beat, scruffy – all talking dogs together. My dog does not feature in the story. She was an Alsatian called Kelly. Her presence allowed me to hear all the open-door confessions and open-heart stories of people, sometimes unkind or even cruel to humans, but never to dogs, always generous, kind, loving and 'everythink' else to their dog children, who loved them unconditionally.

Beryl Gilroy

In memoriam

'Dogs are sycophants and don't know it.'

Mischief, Tawn, Sasha, Kelly my wonder dog and our cats.
To dog lovers everywhere

In loving memory
P.E. Gilroy (1919-1975)
'As long as you call my name I live.'
(East African proverb)

CHAPTER ONE

Finbar and his two henchmen were waiting for me in the park. They had heard that I wanted to buy a dog for company, and they owned a suitable one – an Alsatian crossbreed, small and intelligent. I had only just moved to this part of London with its darkly subterranean life. I wanted a pet, to remind me of the devotion of dear Florence, my wife, who had passed away five years before this warm summer day, a day so full of voices – trilling, skipping and tossing themselves about the park. I wanted something to love and indulge.

It was as if the light in the park grew suddenly brighter, and an inner eye, to help me once again to care for life, opened up in me. Finbar questioned me closely as to the size, the breed, the temperament of the dog I wanted. He tested the depth of my pocket and then sent Jamsey Ned to fetch the dog. Jamsey was a young, London-born Irishman with a head of very dark curls, shoulders lank and frail, but with a soft round face and a pleasant smile in spite of his broken front tooth. He rapidly disappeared and just as rapidly returned with the half-breed (Alsatian and corgi) 'vaccinated for everything, house-trained and obedient'. She was a ridiculous mixture of the two breeds – face, legs and ears of an Alsatian with the body and tail of a corgi.

'She was often mistaken for a foreign breed,' Finbar said with conviction.

'Her nose is phenomenal. But for her height, the police would have bought her,' said Finbar.

'For her nose alone,' said Jamsey.

'All dogs have cold noses,' I observed.

'Of course they do! Of course they do and no sane man will doubt that, but this dog's nose is efficient – hot or cold.'

'You kissed the Blarney stone several times today?' I laughed.

'Been kissing it all my life.'

But my reaction to her was immediate, to her colour alone, steady-brown and short-haired, rather than the dense, springy coat of Alsatians, and as far as I could tell she had inherited only the good qualities of the two dogs that, end to end, had bred her. I had not come prepared for such immediate attention from Finbar and his friends, but I accepted the lead which appeared in a flash from Jamsey's well-worn overcoat, and led the dog away for a little trot of friendship. She hesitated at first, making sounds of protest, but, with Finbar's voice thrusting her on, she regained her composure and walked. I looked back for approval from her friends but they were busy cosying up to the £180 I had just paid them. (Twice the going rate I later learnt.) I walked on, faster this time, fearing that Finbar, the gaffer, would ask for some more. Footsteps hurried after me. It was the lackey, Jamsey Ned.

'She's a bitch and the spaying has yet to be done,' he said seriously. 'Go to the pet shop. Alana in there will help ya.'

'Thanks,' I replied. 'I have to go there anyway to buy some food and things. By the way, what's her name? Has she been named?'

'Sheba. A lovely dog. I watched her grow. What's yours? You never said.'

'Alfred Grayson,' I replied. 'Retired civil servant, trying not to live a lonely life.' At that point I did not feel like telling him any more. That I had always earned a fair wage because I could 'pass'. Nature had hidden my Africa; all that might

8

have made visible that heritage had vanished in me, and most of my family. He did not need to know that I had done my share of work and was now ready to live quietly; that after my wife had passed, a victim of the Big C, the house became too large for me. I felt like a seed in a rattle as I prowled about it, seeking all the old nameless certainties; that finally I had purchased a small made-over coach house, close to Hilburnel Park, local transport and shops. All young Jamsey needed to know was that, starved of company, I wanted a dog, something to call my own, to fill up my time and my consciousness and so forestall the forebodings of a dull retirement.

Although the young man had suggested that the pet shop was some way off, it was really quite close, but there were two busy crowded streets to cross, traffic streaming from all directions. You knew you had reached it by the smell. Used cat litter for one. The dog seemed quite confused. A large window containing a most exciting display of tropical fish and the sign 'Pet Shop' painted on the brickwork confirmed the trade carried on within.

Behind the counter sat Alana, slim, thin-faced, blue-eyed and bottle-blonde; she who would help me flesh out my needs. Her space had been cut out of a larger shop heaped with bijouterie for dogs. Some tinkled in the wind that stirred the smells.

Someone had tried to make a display of essential dog products but found it too hard, so Alana was permitted to recount the stock to each customer in the silly-child, flirtatious woman's screech, on which she threaded her words.

'Can I be of help to you, sir?' she asked in a discord of undulating sound.

'Oh, I'm sure you can. All this is new to me.'

I could hardly see her eyes or the definition of her face from behind the mask of make-up she wore. Then she whispered seductively, 'I do my best when you men come in. You men allow themselves to be informed but then you

9

go right out and spout the undigested info to other men. Instant experts. In my *Woman's Own* recently they talked about two things. The Power complex and the G-spot, which they said dogs also have. I personally believe them because my dog has a big G spot, you know, grudges and that for other dogs. She does not balk at showing a grudge. Just like some women, especially the unbeautiful ones.'

'I'm sure you're right,' I smiled.

'There you are,' she replied, showing her teeth touched here and there with lipstick. 'You see a man's preference for doggie paraphernalia developing before your eyes. And then he goes and spouts this info to other men.'

'You repeat yourself,' I said.

'Yes,' she beamed. 'Sometimes.'

After that, a battle of persuasion and resistance ensued between us and, rather than lose ignominiously, I resolved to concede graciously.

The dog made herself comfortable and snatched forty winks, her eyes still blinking while she snored. Alana, dressed like a dog's dinner, got up from behind the counter the better to display the doggie necessities, all the while wiggling her backside like a worker bee telling the others where the honey could be found.

'Well, sir,' she began in another flood of talk, her voice warm and intimate. 'What can I tell you but the absolute truth? You'll need a bed and a basket for her, some doggie toothpaste, deodorant tablets, bath towels – and have you a garden, sir?'

I nodded.

'Then you'll need a doggie loo, sir, and a poopscoop for when you go out. The loo will have to be maintained and we have various products to help you. We also have health maintenance vitamins, birth control pills and various other delicacies.' She changed cadence and then ran on.

'Do you go to the park, sir? Then you may like one of our foul-weather coats in the colour of your favourite football club, so that your dog could match you to perfection. All these things are contained in our "Good Value Pack", which you can obtain with favoured customer status and a mere fifty quid extra, for £85.87, sir. What you do not use after a month, we may be able to purchase back at half the original cost. We can also provide excellent insurance cover in case of illness. We are indeed a considerate...'

I did not let her finish. 'Where do you keep your consideration? Under this heap of rubble!'

Ignoring me, she banged on the counter very hard with her small claw-like, purple finger-nailed hands, and said determinedly, 'Very good value. Go with the heart, I say. It's the heart that does it. Very strange indeed is the heart.'

My dog woke up, sniffed the air and lay down again. She was patient and resigned. I picked up the items I wanted, paid up and went home, leading my dog. She was inquisitive and stopped to investigate the walk and leave her odour here and there. She was curious indeed.

Back home, we began to bond. I left some of my clothes around to help her forget the smells she had known, and then, rolling my jumper into a ball, encouraged her to 'fetch'. I talked to her about Alana the salesgirl and, when I was right, she wagged her tail with conviction and vigour.

CHAPTER TWO

With the ownership of a lovable dog, I became a man of routine. We woke early and joined other dog-lovers in the park, told tales about our dogs and made friends with those people for whom the park had become home. I had access to the curiosities of all races and ages of people. The dogs were the children many of us had never had, and some days we literally never shared any other stories, except those telling of the life and times of dogs – alive, dead and yet to come. The park was the one safe place where we found fellowship and the privacy to discuss our love for dogs without snide looks or words of condemnation. We laughed and shared and enjoyed.

Many of us faced problems: loneliness, yearnings, needs buried under the skin or combed deep into our faces like tribal marks. Some had lost their homes during the 'Me and Myself' years of the Eighties, others had turned to drugs and became criminals to feed obsessions, while some just walked away from the incomprehensions of their lives.

Some turned to dogs for strength and solace. Wonderful animals who shared human existence, and never tired of being a friend, who knew psychically what was to come; I was sure of that. 'Look, Sheba,' I said. 'Your place! The park!' I surveyed our surroundings, sensing my failure to appreciate their extent – so large yet so intimate, here in the heart of this ancient city that had become a mix of voices from every part of the world. I stared into the distance, trying to separate the park into comprehensible areas – for children's play, sports, flower beds – and then found myself still unable to judge its size, no matter how hard I tried. It seemed enormous, with pale and dark layers, its lighter and darker greens, coverts of sheen and shadows and places where ghosts sat and waited for those who would never materialise.

There was sitting-space and grass on which dogs gambolled and children lolled and giggled, and where hidden ancient fountains, clogged up by time, trickled water that had once gushed. The park ensnared my imagination, agitated my sense of form with its lines of trees, clumps of flowering shrubs and dwarf willows weeping into the lily ponds with their swirling tray-like leaves. In the distance, a tree yielded to the wooing wind. It was called the 'Lightning Tree', and much visited. In a storm, lightning made the weirdest of designs above and around it, wandering in and out of its branches, without ever striking either a summer leaf or a winter twig.

As I got to know it better, I learned to appreciate the parks variety. On grey days, gulls dropped out of the skies; ignoring erratic pigeons and dogs careering round and round like wooden horses on a merry-go-round. Flowers, all different, all articulating nature's calendar, contrasted with the dark-grey, food-eager bodies of courting squirrels and garrulous birds nesting in the hedges. I came to see the park as a living thing with its own vibrating heartbeat.

Each day brought immeasurable pleasures. I was being drawn back to feelings from the dawn of my time, young, crisp, unwounded feelings when life caught me by the scruff, blindfolded me and set me wandering in the jungles of romance and love.

Now, I felt I was coming alive again, the willing recipient of each new day as I went out in dog-given confidence to meet those who had made the park their home, people who were free of ambitions and any expectation beyond the weekly dole cheque. I had, as I have said, gained access to opportunity and profitable employment, at a time when colonialism was still the savage enemy of blackness, by learning to play-down my invisible Africa, making my ancestry even more remote. I had prospered, I enjoyed a comparatively comfortable pension. But unlike my new acquaintances I felt unfulfilled. I had sometimes felt that my absence of dark pigment had dragged me where I did not belong. My tastes had altered, but were they mine? Was my ability to 'pass' really 'cocking a snook' at the bigots? Was I hiding from myself?

But in the park there was no pretence. There I met people who were often more concerned with animals than with themselves. Among them my excellent education was often disregarded. Among them I had at first felt overdressed until I pulled off my tie, folded it neatly and put it in my pocket. We met under the Lightning Tree and made tea in a little hut beside it. To drink that tea – brewed so strong and tarry – I had to learn to change my tastes again.

I became aware of the Finbar behind the role of 'Gaffer' or the 'I'll put you right' authority in the park, as a man with his own vulnerability and hurt, but still a cunning man, astute in his dealing with others. I read his eyes, every muscle of his face eloquent, able to assess people and events with the wisdom of the sages. Every surrounding nerve around his eyes articulated knowing, having, giving – mostly to the dogs around him. Time was shearing his head, leaving it bare at the front, though the greying wisps of hair at the temples gave him a distinction. Dressed in old woollen trousers and an open-necked white shirt, he looked curiously pleasing, even to the fashionable women who sometimes gazed at the men on the benches as if pitying creatures from another planet. His face, rugged but still attractive, must have broken many a heart. He lived alone and whatever his business, it was cloaked in secrecy. The park-keeper (an elderly West Indian who was given to reiterate, 'I seen life! What life I seen!'), would point to Finbar and confess, 'I lets him alone to run t'ings. I keeps out of his way.'

I met Declan and Joe who sometimes loitered in the park. With Jamsey Ned, they made the tea turns about. Others dropped in now and then – like Arabella. She I met almost immediately after I got my dog. Self-centred though she was, I recall her with the deepest feelings of warmth, friendship and pleasure. Her poodle, Honey, was a dirty-white colour, fussy – a demanding brat of a dog. Only Arabella did not think so, and referred to Honey as one of the Creator's masterpieces. The other masterpiece was Arabella herself. But if they were forms of perfection, both owed as much to artifice as to nature. Honey was Dog-woman, and Arabella a theatrical relic. It is said that one human year equals seven dog years, so since Arabella was fiftyish and Honey seven, they were around the same age.

Self-disclosure was never a problem for Arabella, no jump from a mountain top into a gorge: it was a stroll into a garden decked with neon lights, which she could switch on or off at will. Her life story, reinvented for style and effect, was a mixture of mystery, chaos and a desire for independence. Friends said she was related to Oscar Wilde for wit and to Bernard Shaw for sarcasm. I simply thought her a caricature of benevolence, with malevolent touches. When she laughed, she swept the air with her long, brunette-dyed hair, letting it lash whoever was close by. She told us numerous stories of how she swiped her female friends out of existence with that hair, and then made off with their beaux, who eagerly followed her.

While Arabella, a compulsive actress, was fixated on her life on the stage, decades ago, Honey was also a prima donna, but with creeping caudal arthritis. When Honey was in the mood, she wagged her tail in time to Arabella's tunes. Sometimes we sat under the Lightning Tree, watching the blackbirds rise like pebbles thrown from the grass beyond, while Honey barked at them as if her heart would break to see their violation of her territory.

Arabella had seen good days and she picked out the best of them to share every amusing detail with us. Her voice was dated – the received English of the Forties and Fifties and further imprinted with 'class' through her theatrical roles. She was the heroine of all her stories, and never needed much prompting to begin...

'You know, my darlings, I have had the worst experience of my life! My ex turned up after so many barren years. Heavens! I was frozen in my bed and, believe it or not, he joined me there! Removing his clothes like an act of expiation. Whatever he did, he was superficial in his style and his efforts. Very rudimentary indeed! I just could not believe that he had acquired no new techniques after years and years of flirting around. He was personable, but even as a young man he showed all the signs of sexual sloth. We hail from the same sleepy-hollow of a village. He was hard to love. His cup was always half-empty, never half full. I was never in love with him – my love was my strong and yet fragile fisherman – the Adonis of Majorca, where I had gone for a restful hols. *He* was so pleasant – so grabbing – so thorough in all he did. 'I still remember the feel of his arms enclosing me, taking me to the land where the essences of love poured jewels into our hearts. So wonderful!

'We met for the last time under a wide, star-crowded sky, each twinkling and daring desire into us. We lay on the sand with the surf breaking in the distance, and the moon a golden, shimmering stain on the water. My heart fluttered like a bird with a broken wing, and broken were my wings of resistance! My love for him gushed out in flaming desire, and urgently became a conflagration. It only made me regret the brevity of my time there. Love has its splendours, its delights, its rhapsodies! Its moments of bliss beyond words.

'I caught my plane the very next day and returned to London, where a part in a revue awaited me. I bled through my pores like a holy icon for the arms of Ricardo, my Adonis. The pain of loss was elemental and consuming. I wept between shows. My appetite vanished; rings appeared around my eyes and threw dark shadows, which aged me by scores of years! I must return, I thought. But, afraid of my own actions, I lay in bed and would not get up. I donned a gorgeous nightdress, exquisitely titivated my face and prayed for Death to snatch me away. To no avail.

'But then, as I began to tell you, Harold Heyho, euphemistically nicknamed "Heroic Harold", once again visited me. He tried to talk me out of my cocoon of misery.

'"Cheer up, Arabella," Harold ordered in weak tones. "The reviews are good. They have called you 'magnificent'. The critics are ecstatic about you." I raised my head. His dog barked at me, 'Ho! Ho!' like an old man drunkenly laughing. Harold owned a big dog then – Jingles. One could never figure out whether Jingles was a complete idiot or just stubborn. Harold blinked his disapproval of me. "Good heavens, Arabella. You look like death warmed up!" he scolded. "You must do better! Let me help you! Let us go to our 'Ithaca', our place of bliss and belonging."

Harold was a mediocre actor who drowned his sorrows in alcohol. Sulking, I preferred to sleep. Man and dog were both so pathetic!

'I buried my face in my damp pillow, sobbing dirge-like for the loss of my distant love. I heard a kind of rustling sound, which I did not heed. Then Harold spoke again and said, "You may not like the look of this, but it's all I have." I raised my head and there was his pubic "finger" – pointing. A little finger, mind, and the big dog sitting on its haunches observing him looked as if he'd espied a very paltry snack. My roommate always said, "Little thing, little ego". How right she was all along!

'"What are you waiting for, Harold?" I asked. "An invitation?"

'"Oh," he replied. "I take your point." And with those words he crept in uncertainly beside me. He was uncertain from beginning to end. Nothing delicious about him at all.

I was used to wanton, seductive, daring hands and there he was asking for permission. No passion whatsoever! I adore passion!'

She sipped her tea.

'Gosh, it's cold,' she said. 'I hate cold tea.' She emptied the cup on the grass. It was warm enough to cause the earthworm that caught it some degree of discomfort.

'Was he any good?' probed Finbar.

'From time to time it worked. We married to quell his anxieties. To help him do better. Dashed hopes again, I'm afraid. I became resentful of him and tried to get in touch with Ricardo. But news of my marriage had reached him. He married too, gave up fishing and disappeared into the bosom of migrant America.'

She was silent for a while, lost in reverie. Then she added, 'There is something else you must know about Harold. As a young man he was sent down from university for neglecting his studies. He went to Argentina and learned to dance the tango. He is an expert and demonstrates or teaches it at private parties. Showing off his skill is his obsession and main source of remuneration when he is resting from the theatre. Women flock to him and give him exorbitant fees for his tango services. I fell under his spell too.'

She sighed, then shook herself into active reminiscence. 'But to continue. Where was I? Oh yes, I felt shredded in spirit and shorn of the will to live, and then my friend asked me to care for Honey while she went on holiday. When she returned, Honey snarled at her owner, my friend, and would not leave me. She, at least, saw one little virtue in me.'

Arabella kissed Honey several times, while the dog struggled to be set upon her own four feet. Arabella held her closer as if offering the dog her breast and ran on, 'I was angry about everything and so to quell my flaming rage I became a protester. Finbar's cousin Judy introduced me to the Anti-Vivisection Society, and the stories I heard convinced me that, come what may, the preservation and protection of animals would become my cause. It was not easy though.

'I felt so drained by all my efforts. Once I went into the kitchen, still in the throes of my loyalty to animal life. All of a sudden I felt hungry. Without thinking, I made myself a bacon sandwich and greedily ate it, blowing on it all the time to hasten its availability. Then the truth struck me like a club. "Oh dear!" I cried out loud. "This is animal flesh I'm gorging myself on. Well, it's my hunger and not me, the protester, who is at the bottom of all this! I am a bit of a pig so I will have another." And I did. I pretended it was vegetable in its origins.

'Every weekend we protested. It was a social event at which we paraded our beliefs and our dogs. Then one day an evil old sinner kicked my Honey, and called my sweet poodle a filthy dishcloth. That was too much. I swept off my shoe and took it to the sinner's pate. He was a bully but mushy as cooked oatmeal inside. He yelled for the police and they grabbed me very hard, took me off to their torture chamber and charged me with wounding with intent. I was in there for two whole days before Judy bailed me out. When the case was heard, I was sentenced to six months in Holloway – to serve as an example to deter others, the beak said. But that old grump deserved it! He made me violent – which I am not by nature.

'In prison I helped the younger women by entertaining them with my stories. Sometimes I cried. The women comforted me. I was old enough to be a relative to all of them – grandmother, mother, sister and friend. Even the screw in charge of us listened to my stories about the other petty screws, which I made up to console my companions. Our screw was young; she never once jangled her keys while I talked. I did my best. For good conduct I served only three months, but after I was released I was disorientated and forgot where I was and what I had to do. It was better to wander the streets, but being over-the-hill, Social Services found me a room, and I was able to reclaim my dog. At first, I had to bend my elbows a bit to feed her. It was then that Harold, my husband, came back into my life. There he was, standing at the entrance to my room surveying everything. He brought me flowers – it was the height of summer and roses were cheap.

"'You have a comfortable pad, here, Arabella. I'd like to spend a night or two with you."

'The effrontery of the man! I hadn't seen him for months! "I have no room for Jingles, I have to think about that," I said.

"'Oh, you've got it wrong, old girl. Jingles croaked! Died! Caput!"

"'When?"

"'Oh, last winter. I got turned out of my digs and we became street people. One night he ran off and next day was found frozen! Good Lord! I was devastated. I am lost without him. No one to tell my troubles to. Oh, Arabella, save me! We can wrap Honey in your coat! She will be restrained and we could sleep in peace and amity, and possibly go the distance."

'I did not know what to say. I didn't love Jingles, but I could not blame him for loving Harold. Dogs are sycophantic and don't know it. I turned on the radio. Ella Fitzgerald was singing 'You Can't Take That Away from Me'. Harold stood beaten down, with tears in his eyes. The voice got to him. He held out his hands to me; I hopped out of bed and we danced silently for the last bars of that beautiful song. He moved in on me, just after, with the vigorous tactics of an eighteen-year old. "Don't, Harold," I said. "Don't spoil things! Savour the afterglow of our dance. Your dog is in heaven!"

"'You're so wonderful to say that, Arabella," Harold simpered. "I always wanted him to go there. Especially if there's booze about. He loved lapping beer or licking wine."

"'I didn't know you were a believer, Harold. Or that your dog was a dab-hand at alcohol."

'"I *am* a believer! I *do* wish him heaven. I decided some time ago to hedge my bets." He laughed in a manner that made me think he was being tortured with thumb screws.'

She tossed her hair in my direction, pulled a mini-tissue from inside her sleeve and blew her nose, one nostril at a time, very sedately.

'Did Harold spend the night?'

'Of course. Human feelings and "days of yore" raised their ugly heads. Sad to say, he spread himself over the bed like soft butter on toast and soon snored the night away. We really spent an uncomfortable night together. I was so tired I could hardly speak. I sulked. Then Harold turned vicious – the drink, you know – and said, "You're unattractive when you sulk. I have to go. Have you any money? I used up my stash."

'"No. Not a penny!"

'He glared at me and then shouted, "You have! You must have!" He snatched off my bed-covers, searched my drawers, opened jars and tins and then, with a look of the utmost disgust on his face, walked out. I had fifty pounds hidden in my Bible but he did not touch it, probably because at boarding school a bully had forced him to eat the 23rd Psalm in minuscule bits. I haven't seen him since. I'm sure I would have heard if he'd croaked.'

CHAPTER THREE

I invited Arabella to tea. She could not remember my name.

'Alfred,' I said. 'Alfred Grayson.'

'Yah. Son of the colour gray,' she chuckled. 'Not bad in spite of it.'

We walked towards my house and together made the tea. I played a Mozart piece on CD, for which she expressed much appreciation.

Just before she left, she said, 'Alfred, that dog is out of hand. She jumps up and shouldn't. She ignores you and shouldn't. Send her to a training school called Fynn's. It's good, very good. The vet respects animals and they adore him. Think about it and we'll discuss it tomorrow.'

And off she went. I stood staring at a magnificent sunset for hours. Later, staring at the stars, I felt happily grateful for life, for my dog and for knowing Arabella.

I was awakened by the persistent jangling of my telephone. I am enslaved by that invention. Yield to its demands I must, so, one limb at a time, I pushed myself out of my bed to hear Arabella explaining that a job reading 'classics to some Japanese women' had suddenly come up, and she was going to audition for it and would miss the park that day.

I ate breakfast, fed my dog her 'specials' and rang Fynn's at the number Arabella had given me. Engaged. I checked the number. Still engaged. No call-back services at that time. My phone screamed enthusiastically at me again. It was Arabella saying she'd changed her mind about the audition. I explained my difficulty getting through to Fynn's.

She said in a voice I had never heard before, 'Alfred, this is the voice I keep for morons, and although you're far from being one, you must listen carefully to my very wise words... That dog is wayward and she mustn't be. You saw yourself how she ran off with my five-pound note. You called, I called but she frisked, ran rings around us and in the end made the note useless with saliva. That's really unacceptable. Keep on calling the number. She is young enough to be saved. There's nothing worse than an unlovable dog.'

I kept calling. At last success came in a voice I had certainly heard in one of my previous lives. It was none other than Alana, the pantomime artist in the pet shop!

'Heavens! Have you cloned yourself or are you just ubiquitous like the good old English penny?' I queried.

'Nothing of that sort. We're a very compact and efficient organization. But how can I help you? Summer is blooming. The trees are blissfully alive. Isn't everything beautiful?'

'Two things really. Training and spaying for Sheba. Call them beautiful if you like. They are necessary. She's becoming a brat.'

'You've wrecked her. Given her no limits. Now, about training. Do you want to train with her?'

'Oh dear, no. You train her. Brainwash her if necessary. But send her back to me with a different attitude to the world. She wears me out. Had she been a Dalmatian I would have said she's congenitally deaf.'

'Well, you have to get her kennel-ready, which means shots for a variety of possible illnesses. Then there are the "Conveyance to Destination" fees, Boarding and Lodging fees, plus all the different taxes. You only pay the last set of fees if you want her to live in the house with "youmans". The spaying is done after she is trained – a separate bill for that. You should have got that dog insured. I did warn you. You know, Alfred, I simply cannot understand why we do not accept that dogs enjoy food, nookey and fun just as much as their youman keepers. My Robbie, a little terrier, will sniff himself through the pavement if he scents a bitch on heat. That's nature for you. All around us at this time of year! The sky is full of migrants; you can tell the species by the patterns they make as they fly.'

'You know wonderful truths, Alana. So collect my dog on Friday. I'll buy insurance later.'

I duly prepared Sheba for departure and when the van arrived on Friday I watched her leave.

That day, I still went to the park on my own account. Two people, a man and a woman, came that day, one looking for Finbar, the other for Arabella, and that was how I met Harold and Maryanne.

Harold looked unlike any picture Arabella had encouraged my mind to construct. A fairly short, chubby, middle-aged man with an affable face and an amiable manner, and wearing well-worn clothes, he was quite personable in spite of the chronic anxiety in his eyes. A quiet, suppressed man, some years younger than Arabella, I thought, may be eight or nine years younger.

'Arabella is at the vet's with Honey,' I volunteered, after introducing myself.

'Well, if you see her before I do, tell her I need to talk to her.' He blinked rapidly as if closing his eyes against an army of mites. As he turned to leave, his stylish silver-handled cane bumped against the edge of a flowerbed causing him to stumble a little. He gave an uncertain smile and left. A whiff of stale gin punched me on the nose.

I turned to watch some youths playing clever football but then a young, ebony-black woman sat down beside me, and immediately started talking.

'Where are de oddahs den? I come to see dem today,' she said. 'I use to live here, yu know. Hide-an-sleep under dem bush ovah dere! I use to be in a mental house, den one day, dem come and dem seh, "Everybody know you business. Go way from here." So I go.'

She was extraordinary to look at, with a beauty that

24

seemed drawn from all of the most ancient tribes of Africa, but sullied by hard times, like the look of a showgirl from one of the cheap travelling entertainments of the past. Her lovely, velvet-smooth face made me want to reach out and touch her, to see if she was real or just dressed for a pantomime of poverty. She wore layers of contrasting scarves around her head which she held regally as she glanced at me. I guessed she was around twenty-five or six.

'I name Maryanne. They say I mad-head. Yu know me?'

I smiled and shook my head.

'I come from Jamaica. I had good eddication in Jamaica and when I eight years old I come by yah to meet up my mudda. She bring me come.'

She stood up. She wore a skirt layered like her scarves in various colours but haphazard and unkempt, the hem in a tattered zigzag. The bag she carried bulged as if all she owned in the world was contained in it. She was a mixture of old, stale smells and fresh new ones – coffee, orange and beefburgers.

'Who do you want to see?' I asked. 'Finbar will be here soon.'

'I know 'im, when I jus' come. He live in de same house wid we.' She moved flittingly between something like standard English to the 'London Jamaican' used by West Indians to exclude or confuse white people.

'Yu know 'bout me? Dem tell yu? Well, come walk round de park and I will tell yu meself. Yu know nashan talk? Well. If yu doan know you affi lissen an larn. I know good nashan talk. Mek up in Jamaica.' Her shadow looked bizarre on the grass but the slogan 'Black is Beautiful', when applied to her, showed its truth. Why was she in this state?

I followed her round the park. She was eager to continue our conversation.

'Yu know! Is me gran raise me, an sometimes she use to groan in de middle ah de night. She had some sart of hillness an being a chile, I couldn't guess it and one day she die. De chair jes stop rocking sudden, sudden. Me mudda come for de funeral and she say, "Picknie, I kyan lef yu here like stray dawg. Beside, sending barrel after barrel full of tings oddah people no have, mek you too red-eye and wantish." So she dress me in a Sunday dress, white socks and school shoes, put me tings in a bag and put me on de plane wid har fe tek me to Englan.

'When I see Englan I doan like it. I tink it got smoke all over. I cold so bad and I shiver. I start a cry and holler for me gran, but what da use, she dead and gone. Me mudder cover me out with har vice loud loud... "Stap you nise. White people lookin." I holler hard and she shub me pan me shoulder. I keep back de cry and we start a go to har house. "Why you shub me shoulder?" I ask her. She push up she mouth like it was bird beak. She give a long suck teeth.

'She never tell me when we come to the station; she push me to the escalator; dem no have escalator a Trench Town. Frighten mek me shout really bad, but Aunty Janny, which is what everybody call me mudda, press me to de escalator and I didn't fall down, but I so surprise when I come off, I start another scream and me mudder cuff me quiet.

'People come round to watch, and den I see all dey eyes blue, blue, blue like grandma blue bag. I so frighten I scream again an Aunty Janny cuff me again. "My goodness," seh one of de blue-eye people. "Did you see that? She hit that child. Pick on someone your own size."

'Aunty Janny brace her hip and sharpen her tongue wid a lick a spit. "What yu'll know about me? I can do what I like wid me chile; I carry she a me belly bottom nine month, and now yu all tell me what I mus do to har. I jes collect har all de way from Jamaica, and she fraid for dis place and all you starin, and susuin bout me, as if de child is you own. No! Dis ya is me chile, and I can do what me like wid it."

"'Not here, madam. We have laws here," a man said, taking de piss out a me and me mudder. She brace her waist and open she mouth. "White man…," I pat her shoulder to bring her to order. "Now you go bout yu business…" I hug my mudder and we start a laugh up and de blue eyes laugh too. A policeman join de crowd. Before im ask anyting, Aunty Janny seh, "We goin to me house, please. Mind yourself," and de man step outa de way and we walk past. We come out de station and we climb in dis big red bus and de conductar starin us an holler, "Oleight!", which Aunty Janny seh was "Hold tight!", and we come to dis place call Nuttin Hill. Although dey is no hill nowhere, de bus big an dem whities eyein us up. I see de white man doin black man wuk and Aunty Janny sayin wuk is wuk. She say, "Here yu can put Jamaica bus inside dis English bus." I see people starin us and dey look jes like people back home but when you look dem full you see dem white.

'When we reach de house, it was nat a house at all but one big house cut up into lickle rooms, an Aunty Janny live in one room. Everybody choose time to cook and bathe and nobody care bout de place. In de toilet was a big message. It say, "Do not forget to pull de chain." But wahabout people who kyan read? Me mudder didn't have no bed. It had a "pull-out" and when people pull-out, it turn to a bed for two people to sleep in. De room had Aunty Janny knick-knacks an a settee by a fancy name call ottoman. Den I see a man jacket behine de door. Everybody know man jacket, so I eye it up and was jes goin to ask bout it.

"'Doan be fas mouth," Aunty Janny seh. "Remember you is picknie, and picknie sapose to see and doan see, hear and doan hear."

"'Everyting so strange. Everyting so cold, Aunty Janny," I shiver, brr-brr like sea wave water.

"'You kyan cold now. Dis a June. Febewery is no come yet. Lay down, cover yuself wid dis blanket an sleep."

'So I sleep. Sudden I wake and outside look so bright I tink marnin come, and I so hungry. I get up an start a look for de kitchen. I open a door. Dis mus be de kitchen, I seh, but de room had a big bed an a man an a woman was "doin work" in it. He was moanin and groanin. "Gal, yu so nice.

27

Gal, yu so sweet." His voice was laughable and happy an lickleish.

"'Beg pardon," I seh. "Dis de kitchen?"

'De man turn him head rung, slow, slow slow and yell out.

"'Wha' yu want, picknie? Wha' yu doin heh? Yu too peephole. Go weh, you hear! Go wey!"

'I run long de passage, and den I see me mudder shape on de "put-up" bed an a man huggin her and dey fast asleep. It eleven aclack. Hungry mek me tink is day-dawn. I nevah suck me fingah for a long long time, but dat time shame mek me do it. A clack outside went bang eleven time an den I know is eleven aclack night time.'

We had walked all round the park and then sat watching the game of amateur tennis in progress. Maryanne, however, stuck to her tale. The ice-cream van, its bell playing the first two lines of 'Bye Bye Blackbird' non-stop, forced me to offer her an ice-cream, and we took time out to lick cones.

'We will finish the story another day, Maryanne,' I said, oppressed by its intensity and detail.

'You doan want hear bout me?'

'Of course I do!'

'Den we go round again!'

The day was lovely. The thrushes were warbling their satisfaction that their brood had been reared. The black-birds hopped on the grass in dainty steps. The roses and carnations were splendid in their show of colour.

'I miss my dog,' I said. 'Next week she'll be home. I can hardly wait.'

'You know, I never had a pet for me. De dog dem belong to de house, and de house belong to me gran, and so de dog belong to her too. But I tellin you bout me.'

'Yes, of course,' I replied, feeling truly pincered between my wish for Sheba's presence and Maryanne's unending tale.

'I didn know nuttin. She never tell me nuttin but de next marnin, she drag out some new clothes an tell me, "You goin to school, and dis is wha' you affi wear. White blouse, navy-blue skirt an same colour cardigan." I put on everyting but de skirt too long and swingish. It touch me heel and I look like beggar woman in granmother nightgown. "It have to do today. Tonight I will tek it up a lickle bit. Clothes cos' money," Aunty Janny seh.

'When we reach school, I see everybody wearin blue gingjam dress. I start a cry when dey trouble me an call me "immigrant" an "just come"; and de word dem hurt me bad, and I run home. I tek de wrong bus. When I reach de road it tek me long to find de house, and when I get dere a lady waitin fer me.

"'Don't cry," she tell me. "These are winter clothes. You must be boiling in these things. Did your mother buy you summer things?" I shook me head an ask her, "Who is you?"

"'I'm the teacher. Someone had to look for you. I volunteered. Have you a dress?"

"'Oh yes, teacher," an I begin to neh-neh cry again. "Show me," de lady seh, and together we look through everyting and I choose a pink crepe dress dat fit nice. "You have a nice little figure," the lady seh. "Come on. If those beefy girls laugh, tell them what I said."

'I didn tell Aunty Janny cos she doan want nobody to see inside de room. I like de school. We was all "cartolics" and dat had meanin. Faith is Faith. I really glad to go school. When I reach dere a happy girl come inside me, ready to learn, but everyone say I sensitive an I doan know what it mean, and I couldn cure it.

'Den one day I come home an Aunty Janny home. I never fine her deh home! I use to do work till she come. Tidy de room, wash up an all de little dis and dat. But she sit down a cry. I tek affe her for de cryin. We cry easy, easy.

"'Wha wrong, Aunty Janny? Wha wrong?"

'Den she burst a fresh cry, an shout, "Uncle Johnny gone! He tek me money to rent a place and he left me, he say he doan want no belly."

"'Who gettin baby?" I ask her. "Who get belly?"

"'Me," she seh. "Me."

'Aunty Janny had a lot of sufferation. She wuk at a laundry an stand up so much, she foot swell up. I was sorry fer her and had to lissen to all she troubles, but when I was ten de baby done born. She was so busy wid de baby dat she forget me birthday. I remember me granmother an how she buy me a birthday dress an give me a birthday shilling, an I start to feel sorry, an before I can stop it, eye-water start to roll down me face. I sniff me nose an wipe me face. I was ten, jus' ten. I did tink dat it was de cold swell me mudder belly. She stay home a month and den she say, "Tell dem at de school dat you goin back to Jamaica! Tings good in Jamaica."

'So I spread de word an left me happiness school after Chris'mas. Chris'mas no happy time, but people who use to look us cut-eye wish us Merry Chris'mas. Chris'mas here was stale, stale, stale. No John Kanu! No masquerade. No Jump up! And den I find Aunty Janny play a trick on me.

"'You ent goin back to Jamaica yet. You stayin to watch man-baby. I want fe call har Amanda, but me no want any duff-head fe point she an say 'A-man-da – Dat is a man – so I will call har Sensimilla. So you watch har."

"'Me ent de baby fader," I said.

"'You ent dat, but you is Sensimilla sister and you mus' call me Mummy. I ent you Aunty Janny. Me here with me two picknie, Mary an Sensi!"

"'God!" I seh. "People smoke sensi a England and Jamaica… it mek dem disputatious.'"

Maryanne sucked her teeth for five minutes, then continued, "Every day I wid dat baby. I like it but when it begin to wake an holler I couldn play at all. One day I snick out an begin play hopscotch on de pavement. I could hear de baby cry. I give it a long suck teeth. Dat night I feel good. But then Aunty Janny, I mean Mummy, come home wid a new man. I doan like him at all. He ugly. He nose as flat as paper and his mout not only loud but full of cuss an beer.

'I try look after de baby but tha was hard work. I couldn go out. I hide from people who would grass me up to the teachers. I used to sleep wid Mummy on de put-up and den one night something funny happen. I hear de put-up squeaking and shaking. I raise me head and look and dere is Mummy an Mr Musgrove – a fine sight, doin work as granma said to call it, on de bed. Dey took a long time to settle down, and I was wonderin why me mudder like dat work so much. I didn hear de baby cryin.

"'Maryanne," Mummy seh. "Get up. You hear de baby? Get up. You so lazy! You worse-up!"

'When she left to go to work, I was so vex I gave Sensimilla a likkle spoonful of rum bring from Jamaica in her milk and go out to play.'

I laughed. Maryanne laughed. An aeroplane zoomed overhead.

'I been in one a dem. I so frighten I wet meself,' she said. 'You see dat man, Mr Thomack, the park keeper, he mek me remember a neighbour man name Mr Linnister. He was a skinny man but he had fat hands and feet, like dey didn belong to him. He live upstairs from us and one day he die quiet. And dey didn find him fer two weeks. Sometimes he come in me head to cuss me.'

'Why is that?'

'Is me Mummy mek it, really.'

'How come?'

'More and more I start to leave de baby an sit in de park, and when I see children from me school, I hide. Den one day Mr Linnister see me. "You should be looking after your sister! If you leave her alone again I'll have her taken away." He barkin like a dog at me.

"'I beg pardon, Mr Linnister. Please doan tell on me, sir."

"'Then you must let me show you my picture. Come inside. It's magic. It grows."

'So I gave de baby a bottle to suck herself, an den went upstairs to Mr Linnister's flat, and dere he was standin wid

31

he pants down and he willie like a string. "Go on, stroke it. It grows," he order me. He was right. It begin to grow until it get fat and hard. "Now it taste sweet, taste it, as much of it as you can. Go on! It will let you know when it's had enough." I did and den someting like paste come on me hair.

"'You're a very good girl, Maryanne,' he seh, gaspin. 'This is our secret, is it not?"

'Then he voice go huffy. "See, tell no one, do you hear?" 'He dance about a bit and seh, "See, I told you. You make me very happy! Go away and eat your sweets," and by de time me Mummy come home, de baby screamin and I livin by de toilet from eating chocolates, toffee, licorice, Turkish Delight and everytink else from Woolworth by de "pick-an-mix" counter. I tell Aunty Janny de whole story, bout how de old man fool me to empty a bag of sweets in me belly. She had to come home and clean de baby and give it medicine. And she walk upstairs to Mr Linnister. I hear her talkin bout de police an dirty old man, an him beggin she pardon in he shaky old voice, "'They'll send me away. Let's come to an arrangement. I'll do anything you say. Oh, oh please! It's her fault. She should have been in school. She never goes. She made me need company. No one has ever told before!"

'Every Sunday after that me mudder went up to collect pungs like padner money from Mr Linnister, and when she come down she had plenty. One day dead come for him. They find him because he smell. A dead white man don't smell like perfume, yu know. He leave a note. It said, "I have no more money. I gave it all away. I was so lonely."

'We put Sensimilla in nursery, and I was eleven goin on twelve when I went back to school. I go to secondary school an learn some tings. I wonder bout Mr Linnister. He always use to have visit from a lickle boy by name of Joe. As he white like Mr Linnister, I jes tink is he grandson. But Mr Linnister nevah have fren, nevah have party, nevah have nuttin! Poor man. Is life and lonely-ole kill him. Dey bury him an Mummy pray fer him an give him wreath. She say he was bad-head because he never get God in his life.'

'Were you sorry, Maryanne?'

'No, he was too old not to have Jesus in his house, like Aunt Janny.'

'Was it OK at secondary school?' I asked. 'It's a bit rough round there, isn't it?'

'Yes. Plenty of dem worse up since dem jump up and come hey. When dem cuss I cuss; when dem flounce and swing dem tail on me, I do de same. De firs' school nice, Cartolic, but den we got a different secondary school.

'At secondary school there was plenty children come from Jamaica and dey had time to talk and fight over boys, with pimples size of bird eggs on dey face. Some even use to pick em and eat up, but one was a really handsome boy, tall an straight, quite nice and thick black! He name Jules. I used to tink his bones was black too. He had a smooth face an curly hair an he was square build. One day he drop in an tell me dat he goin to study artist-work, and would I please show him my body to see if I would do for his model. Like Mr Linnister, he walked round me looking, looking at me nekked. Then Sensimilla start a cry.

'"You got a baby already?" dis boy ask.

'I shook my head. "No, she me sister. No bady never trouble me, only on me mouth."

'He started coming round every time Mummy went out. He bring his records – all sort, soul, reggae an rock. We dance and den one day he pull me down an show me how love does be, an I believe him an before you know it I got a baby in me belly. I so frighten but I didn't tell Mummy. One day when I get sick she fine out! She gave me a good lickin. ""Yu kyan go ah Maternity. Da bwoy will go a jail. Yu shame me. Oh gawd, how you shame me! I got to pray for you! Yu is a big sinner! Yu kyan see dat bwoy born fa once-a-year, paperbag fader! He doan know nothin. He born in crabhole an dere he will die, a crabhole.'

'Mummy was vex because I bring man in her house, she said. She sent me away to a Mother and Baby house and she never had time to come see me. Everyone dere came from some family wid one or two blind eye. We tink words mean one ting an dey say sometink else. I didn want dat day. I was fourteen almos' when de baby born an Jules bring his friends to see his seed. He never buy toy for de baby. Some of dem plastic-bag daddy buy toy so big de baby han' can't hold it. They want show off. Some seh, "Wha' baby bwoy want with toy?" My baby fader seh when de boy-chile wan play wid sometink, "You bettah give him you bubby". One day I jes split. All strength lef me. People, all sort of people, climb inside me head.'

She shivered a little and looked like my sister who had been stricken with *petit mal*. Suddenly she fell on the grass and started frothing at the mouth, her body jerking and her eyes rolling back.

'Help! Finbar! Seamus, help!' I called out. They came just in time. All the dogs crowded round – whimpering in love and concern for her.

'Put this in her mouth,' said Finbar, giving me a short fat stick.

'She can't bite a stick.'

'Get her pills. Not the red! The blue.' They had seen it all before.

'When she comes round she'll take them. Call an ambulance.'

Maryanne opened her eyes. 'Don't call no ambulance. Don't call no ambulance.' Her brain was confused still, and she rambled on about all those who had bruised her soul.

Rootsman, a black political activist who sometimes hid in the park from the 'Immigration police' or 'Immies', came running and, after collecting her scattered possessions, helped her to a seat. He wore long dreadlocked hair with the fierceness of a lion, but he was very gentle, everyone agreed.

She sat quietly with her sharpened memories, wounded

unto death in the jaws of the unexplainable. The wolves of life had left only the remnants of what was once innocence.

I made my way across the grass and then down the narrow path to my home, wondering if she had been taken to her lodgings. I was haunted by her beauty, so ruthlessly tarnished by suffering. I had somehow ingested her cares and concerns and they had become a disease slowly compelling me to do something for her – to save her. In that brief encounter, she had become very dear to me.

I looked out for her after that, insisted that she was treated with the respect shown to the other women and bought her little treats. I felt for her, for the black in her, by the black in me. I made sure she wanted for nothing and tried to protect her from the crack-heads who cornered her and 'borrowed loot' from her.

CHAPTER FOUR

Later that week a letter dropped on the mat. I noticed FYNN in bold letters. 'Aha,' I murmured. News at last. My poor dog among those relentless creatures who hunt owners for money, like a lioness her prey! I tore the envelope open.

Dear Mr Grayson

This is to let you know that your dog is well. She is down to her right weight and size and we are pleased with her new behavioural insights. We tested her when she arrived, and she achieved such low scores that we wondered whether we should return her as retarded. We do not train 'retards'. However, she has shown some sketchy ability to learn, but will need another week at least if we are to spay her as well as train her.

She still shows 'Chronic Attention Deficit', a lifestyle disorder. This disorder is not intrinsic to the dog but developed because she was given too many commands at once, not allowed to 'hear' what was said to her, and overindulged by frequent and undeserved rewards. Over-gratification is usually the way emotionally starved, lonely and elderly people 'love' their pets.

We will send you a further conclusive bill which will include costs of toys for your dog as you did not

send any with her. Dogs must have toys. Dog toys!
Every serious owner knows this!

I felt criticised and condemned but I held back my desire
to swear. Instead I went to the park and sat on the grass.

After a while Declan, a frequent visitor to the park, and
his pregnant wife, Maisie Mayfield, came by, delighted that
they had been allowed to rent a small apartment from
Beckwell Housing. They had done most of their courting
under the Lightning Tree; their love life was an open secret
to the birds, the bees and the creatures that scuttled through
the grass – as well as to curious teens aching for coitus. Once
Declan had even tied Maisie to a tree to prevent her running
away from him. The police, when called, thought it a lovers'
tiff, and just demanded he set her free. Now they were
legally married and suitably housed.

I promised to spread the news of the couple's good
fortune, and sought out Uncle Nat, a park regular, and
began talking to him about the 'change' that had come to
our two young friends. He was slow at first but he soon
warmed to this subject – his life as change. He took two
quick pulls of his old clay pipe, and then took off like a
clockwork toy.

'I talk a lot, me and me head. I come from one of the
Islands called Plantain Island near Sierra Leone, and I been
living in London since 1950 – I'm nearly seventy-five years
old. Life was hard for me as a young man. I come here as a
sailor and when I come on land I decide to stay dry and
become a landlubber. If I sell by the roadside, the police
come for me, lock me up till next marning and the magis-
trate fine me. I was in jeopardy, left, right and all round me.
One night, cold and fog made me wander into St Martin's
Church, and the gentleman there, Canon Collins I believe
his name to be, helped me with a cup of tea and a warm spot
to sit down. He was a man of big heart and fat compassion.
He helped me get a little gardening work.

'After that I began to get steady work as a gardener and earn money. I married a woman from my country but the weather give her asthma and she went home; she die there. I have a son and he, I believe, is a family man. They don't write me and I too old to write letters. I live in me own accommodation. I am happy. I talk with my thoughts, to myself. I remember. I smile, I cry. When I come here and the squirrels chase one another, the sparrows cheep and the magpies squawk when they see the devil on the grass, and when I feel the wind on my face, I thank the Almighty for bringing me from hunger and want to peaceful old age. Thank the Lord who did not let evil vanquish me. When He call me, I will be willing to go to Him. They will find all my worldly goods in my room. Judy knows everything.'

Normally I am content to listen to such talk, but not that morning. I was conscious of a primeval stirring in my loins for the first time in many years. The old man's voice contained regret and I feared regret most of all. I cautioned myself, but still there was that reassembling of my desire for the physical – caresses, kisses and more if possible. I would not be like Uncle Nat. My body had come to life again, suddenly, surprisingly, thanks to the park and the easy pace of life within it. But throughout all of my reawakened feelings, the unkempt woman on the edge of reality figured not as desire, but as concern. Finbar and Rootsman would certainly know where she was. I spent all day thinking, watching, sitting in the park, wondering how I could save her.

As evening fell, a fiery glow lit the tops of the oaks and the chestnuts in the park and a tease of wind and the early stars made me acutely conscious that my mind was in turmoil. I made my way to Judy's, simply to find out how poor Maryanne had fared. Nobody knew. She was but a pebble in a pool – soon to be lost in the sediment and the slurry. At Judy's, park people had gathered from out of the darkness – every pitch and tone of friendship on view. Confidences were being shared with ease and the certainty of acceptance.

We talked of Maryanne and her plight. The plight of a lonely stranger in a strange land was ours too. She had been abandoned to live wherever she could, uncaring of who lived next door. We felt, we all felt, the anguish of exile – its chaos, its thorns.

Our group had come to share Judy's fire, eat good food and create homely memories in the smells and tastes she offered, as we tried so hard to ignore our 'exile'. The fire roared in the hearth, flickering and flirting in the air like crazed fireflies on a tropical night. Judy toasted buns and crumpets and passed them to eager hands. Even though I was West Indian born, and my forebears had been of Ireland and Africa, at such times I felt an impostor. I hung back, yet they dragged me in. My difference was not outside their conception of brotherhood. The eye is no measure of every truth.

Declan's apology for a moustache shone with melted butter as he drew one toasted bun after another under it. Jamsey loved stylish dancing and was eager to show us the steps, their skill, their precision and language.

'Don't even try,' ordered Finbar. 'Disappear. Put your shoes in a corner. Time for some proper jigging. Clear a space.'

They put on an Irish reel and the dancing, coated with beer and whisky, started. Declan became the comedian and laughter and fun flowed and settled over everyone – even Maisie who looked voluptuous on the sofa.

Suddenly she clutched her side.

'Did any of you hear it? Something snitched inside me! Oh Mother Mary! Save me! Help me!'

The music stopped abruptly. Declan shouted, 'Me loving wife! Dying! While I'm whirling and twirling and dancing for three! Give her the rosary from her purse. Let her hold it!'

'Don't talk about dancing! You weren't dancing – jes making a fool of yuself.'

Maisie was fervently praying, 'Hail Mary, full of Grace. Help me!'

'Don't be such a baby,' roared Finbar. 'You're a big tub of a woman expecting a child any time now. Here's the rosary from your bag and may God help you through this. You're such soft porridge, Maisie, I have trouble thinking of you as a married woman.'

'Judy,' called Maisie. 'Help me! I'm so scared!'

Judy took a discreet look and said, 'Nothing to worry about, love! Your water's broke. Your baby's on the way!'

'Oh Holy Mother! I'm dying! Oh the pain!'

'It's always the same,' coaxed Judy. 'You have pleasure getting it put in, and pleasure when they put it in your arms. The pain is between the two. Soon be over. Call the hospital. You have to be there, Declan; you're the father.'

'Oh no! Not me! Judy, will you go? This is a woman's time. Seeing piglets, calves and lambs coming is more than enough for me.'

With a look of terror in his eyes, he dialled the ambulance. His speech was weak and uncertain, as if he was making a gloomy foray into some incomprehensible land.

'Don't forget the address,' Judy interposed. He waved as if she was many miles away from him. Later he craned his neck at the window to see how close the ambulance was, and although its sound could be heard, he cracked his fingers, snatched up a can of a beer, ripped it open and drank it down.

'Look at you men,' said Judy. 'Your eyes are floating in your faces like weeds in bright red pools. Here's poor Maisie crying out, and you lot, you think her to be suffering pain forbidden to men, so you have to do something to mark yourselves off as men. So what do you do? You drink more cans of beer.'

They managed to help the prospective mother to her feet as the ambulance came closer and closer, its lights piercing the dark. There was little traffic about to impede its progress.

Finbar and Declan slowly walked Maisie to the door.

'We'll take over from here,' said the paramedics. Her moaning still came in puffs and grunts. Declan tried to distract her by whispering, 'Maisie is a daisy, the pride of my heart, I found her in the meadow and only once did we part.'

She gave half a smile, like a cat with only one whisker on a paralysed face, and walked feebly on. The paramedics were gentle and helpful, and at that moment Maisie was certainly being mothered by the men. Judy climbed into the ambulance.

'Don't you want to come?' the tall man asked Finbar.

'I'm too old. It is unknown territory to me. I have him.' He pointed to his dog, Barker, lurking outside in a hardly discernible hidey-hole – a nest under some bushes. He hid when he didn't want to be loved by anyone or lent to anyone for the day.

'Have something to eat, Declan,' said Jamsey. He disappeared into the kitchen and returned with a plate full of appetising food.

'Can't eat a thing,' said Declan. 'When you mix food with your trouble, you get indigestion.'

'I'll leave the plate here,' Jamsey piped. 'I have a meaty bone for Barker when he comes in.'

The house remained frozen and quiet, but for the sound of Declan chewing the food he could not eat seconds before. Judy's sitting-room had become a place where men's imaginations failed them. None of us had ever witnessed childbirth. Of course they had seen animals give birth, but women were different. Another matter entirely. Declan was softly weeping – trying to make sense of the churn of thoughts in his head.

'If I knew how to do it I would do it for her,' he sobbed onto Finbar's shoulder.

'Never mind,' consoled Finbar. 'You'll be a pappy and that's more than I can say. Barker never talks. I know he hates dry bread, but he never says when I give it to him, "Don't give me bread with nothing on."'

The telephone burst in and startled us. It was Judy with the news.

'It's a girl,' she announced. 'We reached the delivery room in the nick of time. Maisie has given Declan a beautiful daughter. Tell the Dad to fetch himself up here and not to forget the chocolates and the flowers, even at this time of night. They sell everything here in the hospital. The mother is very tired.'

A loud cheer followed the slaps on Declan's brawny back. He was silent but the look of pride on his face said everything.

'Now I know,' he burbled. 'Now I know. As soon as she is fourteen I will buy two guns.'

'Poor mutt,' snapped Finbar. 'Thank God, before talking silly.'

Declan, with the broadest of smiles and the happiest heart, left without another word. We sat contemplating his possibilities as a loving, thinking and doing father.

Eventually we started tidying up, so that Judy, on her return, would have nothing to fret about. It was a tiresome and circular task. As soon as we'd washed all the crockery, there was more tea to be made. In the end Finbar and Jamsey got fed up and went home with their dogs; I opted to wait for Judy's return. I fed her dog, Lyds, thought of mine and began to read the Sunday 'rags' Finbar had bought, and pondered the follies of the great, the foolish and the good.

I dozed off, then Lyds perked up, whined a little and went straight to the door. The sound of Judy's key in the lock greatly agitated her. She was beside herself with pleasure. Reassured, she licked Judy's hands and then lay down at her feet.

I apologised for my lassitude, but Judy sat beside me and recounted the events that had taken place. She talked with great zeal of the mysteries of childbirth, the appearance of various parts of the baby and the battle that mothers fought with nature every time they gave birth. It was a good time to ask if she had any children.

'I did have a son but he ran out in front of a car. Dressed in his scout uniform he was. A terrible shock! He was ten! Today brought everything back. That was a terrible winter night. I was beyond consolation.'

She dabbed her eyes and hunched her shoulders in a gesture of renewed despair. I put my arms around her. She jumped alive – her body quickened at my touch. Then I noticed some dark stains down her cleavage and around her neck. I didn't know what to make of them.

Impulsively she stood up and disappeared into her bedroom. When she returned, she was wearing what I thought to be a thin, exquisitely flowered nightdress; but I was mistaken. She sat beside me and pulled open the neck of what was actually a sheer white shift. I gasped when I saw that this was no floral gown, but a body tattooed from neck to thigh with contrasting colours, wonderful in proportion and consummate in craftsmanship.

Words, over which I entirely lost control, dropped out of my mouth and into her lap, well, what there was of her lap.

'How monstrously beautiful! How engaging!' I drooled. 'Was it painful, Judy? Heavens! It's really very imaginative work.'

She leapt in to explain. 'My husband, Ali Ben Ali, was a tattoo artist before he became a prize fighter. I found it difficult to watch him fight every Sunday afternoon that God sent. Bored or tired, he never showed it – I got sick of it. I used to show my tattoos to people who felt fed up like me. He practised on me, you see. He was a very clever man. Very clever indeed.'

I nodded. 'He must have used his scarificator dextrously indeed.'

There was so much I wanted to ask her about illegal prize fighting in that part of London at that time, but I stopped as she impulsively stood up, turning and spinning, deftly

43

curling her body with practised artistry. I caught the comedy of it and laughed loudly and freely. I thought her movements exciting and patted her firm plump backside.

She gently took my hand. 'Come with me,' she whispered. 'Let us unite tonight.'

She began to sniff as if conjuring up the most painful of memories.

'He's dead and gone! I'll never have him back. You will do, won't you, Alfie!'

She took my face in both hands and kissed me softly on my cheeks and then on the lips. Suddenly she held me in a vicelike embrace. I didn't resist. I returned her kisses, her embraces. It was a strong and yet softening feeling without objection from me. She pulled off every stitch of my clothing and kissed me as if she was blessing my body. I enjoyed the feeling of delight, overpowerment and helplessness. The only way of extricating myself was to surrender to her energy and her gratuitous exploration of my person. It was as if she was adjusting to invisible needs. She had a sudden gush of sympathy and desire for me. She was spontaneously daring. The excitement of her touch, her almost fiendish expression of intimacy, thrilled me magically and completely. I had never, in my wildest dreams, thought of Judy as either daring or emotionally sensitive, but she wanted action and there was to be no dallying.

Desired, desirable or not, I rose to the occasion. She grasped my hands, which she said were softer than a baby's bottom, and in a truly intimate manner moved them over her body, while she talked of Dando, her husband dead and gone. 'His real name was Dando O'Dorman, but that was not mysterious enough for his work. He wanted women to drool over him so he changed into an Assyrian man. One of them that came down upon the enemy like a wolf on the fold of gentle sheep. He called himself Ali Ben Ali. When he wanted to trouble me he used to laugh and shout, "Wolf a-coming! Wolf on sheep!" He was stupid like that. We was

44

big in Fairbourn's circus. His act was so good! I don't know which part of this country I haven't seen. We spent some lovely times together.'

'That's nice.'

'And such a time I had minding his cuts and bruises. He needed me, you see! He used to fight everywhere and these well-dressed ladies, at the sight of him gouging and cuffing, would change into spitting cats, hollering and swearing, worse than randy sailors, telling the fighters how to kill. In their expensive mink coats, they forgot themselves and turned to fierce creatures; they was devils, them women. I could never imagine them being loving mothers and tender wives. When Dando my husband, Ali Ben Ali, croaked, I came to London and to hard times. Grass has grown under my feet these past years.'

I was by now teetering on the brink of after-sleep, her voice gentle and lilting to me. Suddenly she began to snore. I got up, quietly dressed, and made my way home.

The night was soft and clear and I was still trying to make sense of the last few hours, conscious only of being tenderly held and loved without fuss – a heartsick man by a love-starved woman, who kept calling me Alfie instead of Alfred. Friendship has its own features – its own sense of reassurance. Like life it is sweet.

Tomorrow my dog will come back to me. Another life, another friendship. That love is also sweet. I felt a tremendous sense of release – the kind of sensation one gets from a lingering bath, a glass of cold water or a slice of hot bread-and-butter pudding. Should I have initiated the encounter? Who knows? In some way I had been overtaken by a kind of starvation, and made good progress through the meal offered to me. I was humbled by the realisation that it was just plain, sensible Judy who had been so loving and tender-hearted, willing to give what she also needed. Quietude lowered me into a deep-down sleep.

CHAPTER FIVE

I woke up early and, because I could barely contain the anxiety of yielding to my desires, the hours passed slowly. I contemplated new possibilities. If I tinted my hair, grew a beard, wore false eyelashes, I could have a good time not being myself – cautious, steeped-in-the-past Alfred. I could become the Touch-and-Go Joe, the Ever-Ready Man, the Libertine! A vision of Judy opening up for me worked on my eyes like pins of sunlight. A thrill ran through me. Would I permit myself repeat performances? I would need new techniques...

I hurriedly decided to remain 'me': Alfred, the sexual no-hoper. I was never one for grasping opportunity by the forelock. After a while I settled down to await the arrival of my dog; I listened for sounds, the slightest of which threw me into a sharpened state of expectancy. I was worthless at everything other men took for granted.

Instead of my dog, a letter arrived in the post. With some apprehension I opened it, expecting another attempt to con money out of me. I read the letter with my mind firmly made up. No more funds!

Dear Mr Grayson

Please forgive our not returning Sheba today as promised, but she escaped the dog-enclosure prior to being spayed. It was feared that she copulated with 'Ranger', a British bulldog, one of our star sires.

We are simply making sure that she was not impregnated. You see, sir, nature will triumph, come what may; and dogs are not rational enough to say, 'Not today, old chum. The keepers are looking.' That dog has been involved in some astonishing escapades. She needs further observation.

Yours sincerely
Fynn's

Fynn's obviously had it all worked out. They evidently despised us outsiders, and were indifferent to the needs and feelings of both my dog and me. I held back my tears and made a cup of tea. In a rage I drank it – far too hot! I howled with pain, squirting tea over my shirt. I swore and rapidly asked God to forgive my vile utterances concerning Fynn's, myself and the situation.

I was truly disappointed, but pups I did not want and, rather than face Judy's desires a second time, I set out to find Arabella, who understood life in all its moods. I strode through the park and a most magical sight caught my eye. Rootsman, the elusive Rasta, was having his morning run and to see him was to witness a sublime rendition of movement as poetry. He simply flowed through the air interweaving himself with the greenery, the dance of the flowers in the wind and the various musics of nature. I watched him until he stopped to do his Tai-chi routine, and after it was finished, he gathered his long hair and his spirits about him and sat down at peace with himself.

'Hey-man,' he called cheerfully. 'How so?'

'Where's Maryanne?' I called back.

'Who wan fe know? I got har by me house. The bad bwoy dem want fe capture har and ship har out.'

'Why?'

'She bruk-up the hastel again. Dem upset har, mek har upstart herself, and she doan stan fe dat. So I have har at me

47

place. We affi give Toby many pung fe married har and keep har hey. She no have de right paper so she ave to go. It too much fe pay, but Toby want fe buy BMW. Dem bwoy call dat kyar Black Man Wheels.'

'Are you saying that all the years she's lived here nobody bothered to check her papers? And this Toby wants money to help her? I'll help her.'

'She no want help from White Man!'

He shook his head as he spoke.

'Toby say married is a trap and he want money fe divorce if it no good. Maryanne mother look after harself, Sensimilla and her husband. She did give Maryanne to the "Social". Too much black people think "Social" is grandmother house. She have trouble with "Social" plenty year. One time they lock har up, drug har up and keep har till she no know she head from her arse. Me, Dec and odder people wid consciousness go try to save har. We had banner and everyting, "Save Maryanne", "Free Maryanne" and when we go near the hospital, a doctor come out and say, "You thar! What do yoo want with Maryanne? She's a decent gal. Not one of yoo! Teke yourselves awf befoh I call de police." The man was so speaksey-spokesy we bus a laugh.'

I was pleased at least that Maryanne was safe.

'The shops say it soon go be Christmas,' he said. 'I don't like dis time a year. We keep Kwanzaa. Not so much waste-money. Africa-talk and food, man, everyday till time done.'

We sat side by side saying nothing, then abruptly he swaggered off, snakes and whips of hair lashing in the wind.

Under the Lightning Tree, I reflected for a long time upon my current experiences and adventures. I went home with a larger than normal need for little Sheba's presence. I made tea and sugared it well. The telephone again! It went on and on until at last I answered it. Thank heavens! Not Judy this time but Arabella. She began at once.

'Did you see me on the box, old chap? I was in full view of the nation. The reporters asked me a tricky question and, like a politician, I fudged and prevaricated, danced about on tiptoes and smiled. "Make what you can of it", I said to myself.'

'What was the question?'

'Ask me another. I just smiled through my bit about the theatre and how unjustly old actresses were treated. I will have tons of letters agreeing with me. Have no fear. I didn't say much.'

'When are you coming this way?'

'I lent Harold all my money so I'm skint.'

'Have you been in contact with Judy?'

'She rang to...' I nearly dropped the receiver, thought about pretending that we had been cut off. Did Judy tell? What if she did? There was a long silence at my end.

'What's up, old chap?' snapped Arabella. 'Judy rang to say that Declan's child will be christened Theresa.'

I was relieved to think that my caper with Judy was still under wraps. Actually, I felt quite faint to think about it. But it had been good – delicious in fact. I must change, I thought. Become more masterful. Cut, thrust and parry like the men I once knew back home. I must initiate encounters and practise hard.

My dog arrived as promised on Thursday. She was in fine form and extremely friendly and self-assured. But the diagnosis of near retardation rankled, and I was determined to observe whether she could reclaim her territory and her toys. I opened the door, let her in and watched. Not only did she head for her basket, but searched for her indestructible cat and found her ball from a previously untried hiding place. I was absolutely delighted with her, and kissed her firmly on the nose. It was then that I noticed the note she wore on her collar. I tore it open.

'Warning' was written across the top in large red letters, and then: 'Do not overfeed this dog. Dogs are scavengers and have a tendency to gorge. To encourage gorging is to displace your own greed. Respect this dog. Reward it only when necessary. Love this *dog. Do not practise any primitive behaviour upon it. This dog has a soul. Do not betray its trust. Remember dogs are psychic, and can possibly protect you from the evil forces which humans contain. Do not victimise this dog by blaming it for your day-to-day failures.'*

The cheek of those fiends – mercantile, exploitative, intimidatory and full to the brim of shit! Fancy rapping good old codgers like me on the knuckles. My sole reason for having my dog was to love it. To care for some animal that would want me to care.

After that, my rage needed calming. I drank some lemon and ginger tea which Finbar said was good for you at times of impending anger or violent rage but, still feeling sore at Fynn's, went out into the open air with my dog.

Not one of the old brigade was about. Like our contingent of grey squirrels, now silenced by the weather, they were probably hibernating. We made a second tour around the tarmac path and came to the secret heart of the place where the lavatories and washing facilities were locked against those who needed them most. The trees to be chopped down advertised the date of their execution and the benches, from which the seats had been surgically removed, looked ravaged. Even the Lightning Tree was doomed. It was branded a hazard and sentenced to death. There were goodbye notes and prayers on it. There were also pledges to save it, to uproot it and plant it on the Heath so that it could be loved for ever. And then I came to our shed which sheltered us all from rain and snow and cold winds. I read with mounting consternation:

'This shed is to be demolished due to improper, undesirable and unauthorised use.' What use?

The notice had obviously enraged three people who had answered back:

'What is wrong with a little-bit-of-the other with a condom on?'

'I don't like to F-in ask for permission to F-. I can "break in" to any bird I like.'

Is 'breaking in' still a euphemism for rape as it was in my

youth? Real men could not bring themselves to use such a word. Heavens, some things never change.

'Willie has never complained, thank you.'

I sat down, discovering uncomfortably that the now ravaged seat was only half as wide as my backside. More graffiti caught my eye. To the park people, graffiti was self-expression. We saw no harm in its witticisms.

'Cross the road if you see the chicken.'

'Confucius he say the place to catch a jumping frog is in the air.'

'If you want to kill a man, hit him with a loaf of soda bread.'

Laughter poured out of me. Only Arabella would appreciate the graffiti as I had done. Minutes later she appeared.

'I just thought of you and there you are,' said I.

'The people who run this place are such bad eggs,' Arabella replied. 'They delight in giving us helpings of hard cheese. I can't believe they are about to destroy so much. Even that beautiful tree that lightning so dearly loves is doomed. You should see the camaraderie between that tree and lightning. Wonderfully uplifting and spiritual! Makes creatures believe in heaven and hell! Hell again! It's raining.'

A drizzle drained through the dark clouds and several people walked into the hut to shelter. They included a woman about three feet in height and her husband, a good five and a half foot. The silence thickened as they entered the hut. They were outsiders.

'Hello,' said the tiny woman. 'Don't stop talking on account of us – Tiny Dot, alias Sophie, and this here is me husband, Benny, ain't you, Ben? We've known Nat for years. They was in Pentonville togevver. Ben for parking where he shouldn'ta and Nat for sellin where he shouldn'ta. We was glad to see Nat again. Nat sent us 'ere.'

'Yes we are,' Ben replied in a gravelly voice. 'We are travellers parked on waste ground close by. The Council are doing their best to kick us out. Where do they want us to go? Soon you all won't have this place. Pity, ain't it.'

A virulent outpouring of abuse against 'They' and 'Them' followed.

'If I knew who *they* was, I would fetch myself along and give em a kick that would crease them up like paper fans.' A mixture of approving nods and grunts followed.

'Hey, hey, hey,' rattled Uncle Nathaniel, now standing by the door. 'It won't do you no good. Not only do the poor pay more, they suffer more.'

'Hear hear! to Nathaniel and his words,' said Sophie. 'My Benny can bear witness to that and all, can't you, Ben? We've known Nat for years. He was in Pentonville with Ben, wasn't you, Nat?'

'Yes, me old china, I was. They wouldn't get the better of us.'

She grabbed his hands and lovingly squeezed them.

Arabella sat clutching Honey while telling us that Sheba, quietly lying under the seat, was changed 'in a funny sort of a way'.

'I can't pinpoint it directly, but I do believe her to have been desensitised.'

'What do you mean?' I snapped. 'How can a dog be robbed in that way?'

'Simple. They just help her to forget those responses she has unsystematically absorbed from her chaotic environment. And with the best will in the world, Alfred, you are a bit harum-scarum.'

Without making a song and dance about it, Sheba had grown older and with age had come independence.

'Of course she has changed,' I countered, 'She must! She has lost her reserve and is much less dependent on me. In fact, she leads me where she wants to be and when off the lead she is as inquisitive as any monkey, but answers when I call.'

'She does not answer, she comes,' Arabella said, as if sorry for me.

Sheba had an unreformed tendency, however, to follow anyone for a crunchy sweet – any crunchy sweet would lure her away from the finest dog biscuits. To no avail, I discouraged people from feeding her such sweets. She definitely had been taught to crunch in a greedy, famished way.

One day I smacked her and shouted, 'No!' after she begged for sweets.

Some children playing on the grass were shocked when I did this and Sheba yelped. One asked, astonished, 'Did you see what he did? He hit a poor innocent dog. Don't hit that poor innocent dog. Give it to us. We will be kind to that poor innocent dog.' The words sounded like a poem.

Shame scorched my face like flames. 'Sorry,' I replied.

'Don't apologise to us. Apologise to the poor innocent dog. We could tell the police of you. You're cruel to animals. You hit them.'

They frightened me out of the park. I waited for the police and the RSPCA to knock and remove the dog but as the hours passed, and nobody called I was able to relax.

The very next day a rather unkempt and shifty-eyed young man with bleached hair came into the park. He wore grubby jeans and a tacky T-shirt with 'Shit Happens' on the front. At once he began making friends with the dogs. His favourite political beef was 'social justice'. Few of us knew what he meant. For one reason or another, we did not pay much mind to any kind of justice. We expected none. In a monotone, he would begin, while rhythmically slurping his complimentary cup of tea.

'Social justice, mate, is what this country needs. We could do with more social justice. You know I have to work to keep myself in college. Real hard time, man. Social justice was what Karl Marx was on about. To each according to his need. And man, do I need? I need, man. I need money for fags and my rent and my books and birds. I need to spread, man! God, man! Hell!'

He was like a Catholic schoolboy trying hard to use forbidden and shocking words.

'And as for my college! Anything goes – once they get the money, hell, man! Read my shirt!'

We grew tired of that voice breaking wind in our ears for nearly an hour and Finbar, who always spoke his mind, advised, 'Take a turn with the dogs round the park, Mr Darwin. And then you can meet social justice and find out his intentions.'

'You know my name?'

'I know everything and everyone. Is your name Mr Shit Happens?'

'Yeah, man, my name is Darwin Felton. It's a good stick, man! Sure, I'll walk the dogs.'

We watched them go. He started off with five dogs but two walked away, and another two started snarling at cats on the other side of the fence; then he began throwing sticks for Sheba to fetch. She was enjoying herself. I took my eye off her for a single minute – no more – and when I looked again, she and Darwin had vanished.

I was beside myself and, I am afraid, called him a crypto-human idiot. I gloomily pondered all the permutations of that idiot's action.

'I knew it,' said Arabella. 'I did not buy all that garbage about social justice.'

As I recalled his words, my anger began to smoke and then to flame. Darwin the abductor couldn't have gone far with Sheba. This must be the beginning of change for me. I must confront Darwin – now.

As I walked through the park I recalled what a whipping I would have been given for causing adults to worry. My uncles were shark-fishers, tall men, owning strong huge hands with mountainous knuckles. I recall the smack my Uncle John gave me for hitting a donkey and urging it to go faster. Darwin needed some time with him. I emerged from the park to a stream of raucous voices. I looked in both directions for Sheba. In my panic, the rush of cars, the pounding of footsteps and voices confused me even more.

To my horror I had wandered into what Finbar called the crap ground. I scraped my shoe on the edge of the gutter but driven by the need to recover my dog I stepped right out on to the street without thinking. In an instant someone angrily pressed a horn and yelled, 'Why don't you fucking look where you're fucking going, you senile old wanker?'

'Alfred,' said a voice behind me, 'I'm coming too.' I blushed and nodded.

'You're not a senile old wanker but a semi-young go-getter, ' Jamsey said. Don't feel hurt.'

I *was* hurt. I had never been called senile before. All kinds of ideas to ward off senility flashed before my mind but I decided that senility, like age, is a state of mind.

CHAPTER SIX

I started down the high road accompanied by Jamsey, who was suddenly in an irritated and explosive mood.

'I'll kill the bastard when I get my mitts on him. Drat and double drat to be sure,' he muttered. 'Darwin I mean.'

'Go back to the park, Jamsey,' I said, 'and see if he returns. Remember we're nonviolent. Don't lay even a thumbprint on him.'

I watched Jamsey go and then went towards the stalls and there they were! Darwin sat at his 'patch', hat upturned, calling out to passers-by: 'Any spare change, mate? 'Elp the poor, mate. Do you good to 'elp me.'

Behind him a group of zealots preached the Old Testament. The Nation of Islam evangelised. A reggae ghetto blaster played hot tunes. A man, drunk as a lord, sang, 'Yummy, yummy, yummy, I got love in my tummy, and I feel like loving you, and you and you and you,' as he pointed to the young and lovely ladies passing by.

I stood angrily in front of Darwin, while Sheba took bites out of a huge hamburger a caring citizen had offered from his car window. It was as if my baby dog had never been fed in her life.

What do you think you're doing?' I snarled. 'Thou shalt not steal.'

'I just borrowed your baby, man. Didn't think you'd mind. I often borrow dogs. Get real, man! This is the day.'

'And what if she'd been a child? Would you have sneaked off with her?' Quite unconcerned by my presence, Sheba continued to eat.

'No good, mate. Kids is bad for business! People want to talk about them, see whether they're fat, thin, black, white, girl, boy! And where did that kid come from? And then they decide you're up to something and give little or nothing. People love dogs. They bring wonderful gifts for dogs, and a nice friendly mutt like this can do a lot for me. We ain't been here ten minutes and I took over five quid. Pigeons shit in your eyes but you don't care too much.'

'How do you do all this collecting?'

'You just love your dog, man. Talk pretty about it. Act like a doting father, man. Don't be a "naus". They make me sick.'

Sheba wagged her tail. I took her lead and, thinking dark thoughts, left with her. Behind us a voice rose:

'On a hill far away
Stands an old ragged Cross
An emblem of suffering and shame.'

Darwin was one of a species I had never met before – all mouth, long legs, narrow shoulders and a skinny back-end. Quite honestly, I didn't know what to make of him, even as he joined in the singing. His blatant lack of concern for my feelings about the enticement of my dog rankled, but since I had returned with Sheba safe and well, no one else dwelt on what had happened. To them she had strayed, that was all.

But the incident tipped me into a dark mood. The sudden fogs of November; my uncertainties; Darwin's attitude and the resentment he provoked in me: I loathed them all. Dark clouds were either biting their jagged teeth into the head of the horizon, or sometimes resting morosely on its shoulders. Dark, damp days hurried by and then the Fifth – Guy Fawkes night – when whole families celebrated by burning a religious dissident, celebrating his capture and torture, and indeed his terrible death. Night became a time of dark deeds when pets not safely locked indoors faced fire, their primeval fear. Fireworks, loaded in the pockets of a Guy Fawkes replica, leapt out into the darkness as his cries for mercy must have done. All watched with glee, regardless of the animals roaming around unattended. Whole families eating chestnuts and baked potatoes applauded the bonfire in our park, and voices exulted, 'Cor, look at old Guy! Let him burn!' Afterwards, we came into our own and discussed the dynamics of fireworks and burning at the stake. We could not understand how religion could produce such spite.

As November passed in gloom, the early Christmas trees, laden with glitzy baubles, ribbons of tinsel in gaudy colours and unlit candles, appeared in the supermarkets. 'Not this early,' I thought, as children pointed out all the boxes of toys and electronic gadgetry they had ordered from Father Christmas. 'Although I don't believe he exists, Mummy,' an oily Alex said. 'After all, no one believes he is a wizard, and yet he changes shape and size so often. How can Father Christmas do all that work in one night!'

I had thought that all through my childhood, but had kept my doubts to myself.

I patted my dog on her head. 'Isn't it wonderful you have been disallowed speech?' I said. 'Isn't it wonderful you don't talk like these brats that hang around Christmas trees long before they should. Good girl!'

I was suddenly so pleased with my dog, I allowed myself to become invaded by memories of the past. The way it was. The way we were. But what was it about the way we were that now afflicted me? I couldn't tell just then.

And then suddenly it dawned on me. It was the habit of noticing nothing but work and its extensions. I had woken up, gone to work, come home, eaten my meals, made love to my wife, slept and did it all again, day in day out. Living was a circular activity that went on through thirty-two years of marriage. My real needs – and no doubt Florence's too – had passed by unnoticed.

Now my dog made me notice the nuances of life, its rhythms and its changes, and left me in a state both of elation and confusion. I was finding where only 'myself' existed, and I felt both refreshed and disturbed. I knew then what drew men and women and children from the womb to live like maggots in the open sores of the world. Confusion and self-sacrifice! All created by routine dependence on work. To measure time and life through work while linked to all other creatures by indifference and unconcern! But then I realised that even retirement is work. Alone like a stone in a sack, living through the hours and the days. I blessed my dog; in fact, I felt an expansive tenderness to all her kind.

The weather became truly foul. On some days the silence in the park was neat and clean like a cut in a sponge-cake. People talked of snow but it was far too cold for that. No birds sang. A few pigeons fussed, and in their compulsive search for food pecked mercilessly at everything. The water we put out for them froze after a while. The flower-beds fell sound asleep, blanketed under sodden, dead leaves. The jobbing gardeners waited for the weather to break; instead the frost took over, hanging in distorted forms even from the Lightning Tree, and glistening like spume under its roots.

Sheba refused to leave her basket, and in the end I was compelled to buy some foot-muffs for her and force her to walk out for exercise. Barker's rheumatism flared up and he had to be kept indoors and nursed; Finbar was deeply concerned over the welfare of his dog, although insisting that nature had adapted all dogs to cope. Our interest in Christmas was placed even more on the back-burner while we fussed over the sick dogs.

Some relief in our gloom came when Arabella dropped in with Honey wrapped up in a fur shawl the dog had pinched from a sophisticated woman passing through the park. Honey had refused to 'yield' to Arabella's command.

By the time she sulkily returned the shawl, it was useless to the woman.

'This will cost you! Why don't you put that dog on a lead? Here, let her eat it. I don't want it.' The woman had been furious. Arabella had used all her theatrical skills in making her apology. Patiently she had explained that Honey thought the shawl was an animal, and had obeyed her God-given instincts. Arabella had grovelled. A genuine mistake. Apologise on bended knees. Arabella was persuasive. 'Come on, let's put it behind us and go forward as friends.' And the woman had accepted and just to show there was no ill-will had gone with Arabella to Judy's for coffee. There Arabella had introduced her as an old friend just met in the park, and bound in friendship by the love of dogs. The woman had introduced herself as Lucy McAlpine, née Thistlewood – as if she expected the latter name to be known to all the world. She soon became another pair of ears for Arabella's stories and even sought her company for a weekend in Paris, which Arabella regretfully declined. She was still a sophisticate and would need several chic outfits, and she was really down on the doormat financially.

CHAPTER SEVEN

Unlike Arabella, Judy, always the generous hostess, suffered no delusions of grandeur. She was solicitous and caring. She graciously welcomed Arabella's guest and quietly went about including her in our communal Christmas preparations. She and Finbar had been given permission to hold a carol service in the park, weather permitting, and had advertised their intention to do so within the community. It was also to be our farewell to all that was to be demolished in the spring.

A week before the event we met to arrange the programme. Our local Council was even going to provide, erect and decorate a Christmas tree, and light it by way of power from Judy's house. They generously supplied the connection to our tree and we were delighted and grateful.

As the day approached, we, like the children who passed through our park, were elated and expectant; the dogs also caught the mood and were friendly and sycophantic in the extreme. Some seniors said they'd lend their voices, and assured us that they would heed the weather and dress suitably. Judy and Finbar provided what Arabella called 'the tuck', and for once the weather remained cold but dry.

The Christmas tree was resplendent with baubles gleaned or snitched or conned from Mr and Mrs. Everyman; and the lights twinkled in the dark. We sang our carols with all our hearts and shared the full meaning of the singing with friends and family, near and far. It was a loving time. What added to our joy was some welcome news. Unknown to us, the chief brigand, the Supervisor of Parks, had attended our little ceremony of farewell. Our commitment had touched his heart, and the doomed life in our park had won a comprehensive reprieve. Although we were not party to the details, we were overtaken by a delight which warmed us through. Only Arabella felt differently. She stood alone beneath the Lightning Tree and said how angry she was at those faceless people who made decisions for the whole wide world. She meant for the park. We distributed our presents and thanked our Creator and went in a bunch to Judy's where we discussed the ceremony. In the midst of enjoying the food, the door burst open and in from the darkness staggered Darwin. He appeared to be in the grip of a demon known to us all: the Demon Whisky.

'You bastards. I'm not good enough to be invited! I'm hungry and here you are all stuffing your faces! I hate you dogs and bitches!' and he fell to the floor.

'He's drunk as a lord.'

'He's not drunk. If it's not weed, it's speed.' Finbar grabbed him by his legs and dragged him out of the living room and into the kitchen. Judy threw a blanket over him and left him to sleep it off. From time to time someone wandered out to see if he was OK. He began to cough and retch. We put him in a sitting position and left him there.

'Had he been a dog, he'd have felt an illness coming on and instinctively ate grass. But as he's human, he prefers to vomit and enjoy the smell,' said Finbar who could not stand such performances. 'My priest would call that behaviour the manifestation of unfaith.'

The sight of Darwin so out of control had made me feel helpless. I was touched by his youth and his lack of care for himself. But just as I was leaving, Mrs McAlpine arrived. Judy had invited her to join us for supper. She looked seductive in smooth electric blue, and the merest whiff of the scent she wore grabbed me. I knew that scent. Florence loved it but I couldn't put a name to it. It rose above Darwin's stale alcohol and made the smell tolerable when Judy all too briefly opened a window.

There was a frozen stillness about Lucy McAlpine, the fixity of a gouache painting. No laughter, just smears of subtlety. I was sure I had seen her before. She stared at me too, as if trying to dredge up my identity from a place deep down inside her. Everything about her had been set in the aspic of respectability from days gone by. She was the kind of woman who would maintain her propriety without any concern for its effect on others. I felt like snatching her and rushing her into the present; standing her on her head, her garments falling in reverse to show her that not even the wind would stir at the sight of her legs.

Yet she was attractive. A particular woman who would warn, 'Sex if you like – every Sunday after meals, but no messing.' There may have been clues in her behaviour which would have revealed her inner landscape, if one knew where to look. I didn't care to look, and in spite of the pleading note in Judy's voice, I decided to leave.

'Goodbye, Alfred,' she wheedled. 'Remember. I *would* like a nice Christmas gift from you, Alfred.'

'You'll have to tell me exactly what you want in very simple words, my dear,' I replied, gently rubbing the back of her hand.

I took the long way round the park – fearful of being mugged by itinerants like Darwin.

Home at last, my mind kept flitting from one phase of my life to another. The God of sleep reluctantly ignored me. At around midnight the memory swam out of my unconscious and I recalled just who that woman was!

She had worked in offices close to Florence's, ages before we were married. She was a teenage secretarial assistant and then we heard that she had been snapped up by one Jacobus McAlpine, old enough to be a senior uncle. They had disappeared into the wilds of Kent to rear mink, which all the chic women of the time wanted to wear. He subsequently ran off with another woman, just as young as Lucy had been when they married, and now here she was, his ex-wife, stiff-starched and particular. She seemed never to have been young in the way of other young women and, settling for a life of stiff disharmonies, had allowed the melodies which enrich the lives of others to pass her by. She did, though, now have a collie, called Mutt, which Judy had persuaded her to buy.

I kept my knowledge of her to myself, and watched her as she breezed through the park to go slumming on our High Road. In my head I referred to her as 'Prim Particular'. From time to time she popped up out of the corner of my brain but then disappeared again. Her face was not particularly memorable, but it displayed intriguing suggestions of care, concern, with undercurrents of overcontrol and 'I don't like it very much' – although she never named the 'it' she disliked. She began to haunt me and I found myself thinking of her at moments when I shouldn't have been, moments such as bed times, or taking a shower, or when eating a cold fried egg. Once or twice I even stopped drinking my tea, all the while sneaking glimpses at her form through the railings as she made her way to the shops. I was curious to find out what she was truly like. I faced Christmas with a definite need to know.

Christmas passed quietly, with old memories, but without that knowledge. After Christmas the weather grew worse. It snowed and there is nothing like snow to keep people indoors. The park died. What was left of the seats rotted. Only hardy teenagers ventured in. It seemed as if the park belonged to us dog owners. The silence was frighteningly articulate.

Gradually, Persephone, the Spring Goddess, began to touch the earth again. Those trees and shrubs programmed to flower burst into blossom, at first timidly and then profusely – cherry, almond, apple; and the wonderful magnolias spurted out of their buds as if by magic. The jobbing gardeners returned and began to destroy and shear the hedges, so throwing the park open to everyman's gaze.

We lost our privacy – the support of our camaraderie, our closeness. The eyes of the smug and the bigoted were continually upon us. However, we were still able to brew good, strong tea and continued marinating our teabags in either evaporated or condensed milk.

Spring sneaked on. Trees began to show larger leaves and the sticks of branches to grow fresh green flesh.

Everyone came back to known tasks. Voices rose and fell again. The joggers, the children, the dogs returned. There was the pleasure of the familiar, and then one morning whom should I see dancing through the wind? It was Rootsman, but all his locks were gone. He was as bald as a football.

'We missed you,' I said. 'Finbar was worried about you. Where's your hair?'

'I been hidin, man. I don' belong here. I come here fi spend last Chris'mas with mi frien', Eden. Before I turn rung, another Chris'mas come grabble us. I did get a lickle wuk but de bad boys dem ketch me. I slip out of de cage where they put me, and now I doing me ting again. I sarry, man. I have to be a ball-head. They looking fe man wid lacks. You know, a pelice ask me ef I know "Root", a man wid lacks. Me gran'mother, queen Lizziebeth, disown me. And feisty, bragadocius Maggie too – all a dem disown me.'

'Any news of Maryanne?'

'Yes, har mudda come take har, carry her go Jamaica. Sensimilla is a big child now, fat and strong. She too in Jamaica. Mary is a nice, eddicate woman, you know, but dis country disown her too.'

'You mean her mother came to fetch her?'

'Yah, man. She seh the grandmother jumbie nevah let her res', never let har sleep, till she carry Maryanne go home. Mary nice, you know. If I feel like fallin in love, I will look her out.'

The last time I had seen her she was in the Lassbery hospital, identified as Maryanne Jamaica. She was full of pills, but listen as hard as I could, she did not rattle. I was so glad, so glad she was free. It had worried me that she'd become a victim of the system, filled up with one semi-lethal drug after another and then ejected to live in 'The Community' yet again.

If by 'community' was meant our park, then the word had some meaning. It was more than a rendezvous, more than a place to lose one's armour. It was the place in which we wore robes of a classless humanity – where a man or a woman was judged by an appreciation of the decent, the right, the worthwhile thing to do. But in the world outside the park, it seemed there were only individuals – as our prime minister once infamously proclaimed – pursuing their own interests. The park gainsaid that terrible creed of economic selfishness. At its heart was our relationship to our dogs – and through them to each other.

We could not deny them their rights as we had been denied ours. Only Rootsman was sure of his ground and protested on behalf of everything that had a face. He said, 'Nah me, man. Me got rights. I is white man burden. White man bring come-carry-go black man, chiny man, coolie man to plant rice and sugar and cotton and tabacca fe sell. Nobody trubble dem. Why dey trubble everybody, hey! Ancestor blood deh pan dem han!'

'So you're sure Maryanne is OK?' I continued.

'Yah man. She wid her mudda and har mudda got a good business selling obeah fi tourist. Dem call it charm.'

He ran off and out of the park so suddenly I was almost sure I had imagined it all. But life itself creates mystery, calls it by tantalising names, and we hapless mortals join in and make it our own. I hitched Sheba to her lead and went for a stroll beyond the park. Even if that wilderness contains predators that roam abroad and sometimes overpower us, how can we be certain of our place of safety unless we sometimes leave it?

CHAPTER EIGHT

The high road was vibrant, heaving, frenetic! I passed shops that had gone sales-crazy. Signs advertising various commodities were emblazoned across shining glass windows, giving them a bizarre hilarity. I could not resist the impulse to spend money. I wandered into the confectioner's and bought a rather over-decorated box of chocolates, meaning to go straight round and surprise Judy. I was outside the shop and bent down to unhitch my dog from the rail when I felt a gentle tap on my shoulder. I looked up into Lucy's face.

'Hello, Alfred,' she chortled. 'You're out early.'

'So are you, Lucy. You should "leisurise" your mornings.'

'Leisurise? You're not going to have me kill myself, are you? I've used up every spoonful of coffee and a cup of that drug sets me up for the day. Dutch coffee, which I adore, is ten per cent off today.'

'There's a coffee shop across the road. Let's have a cup.'

She did not reply at once, but her facial muscles tightened. I could see that she was thinking.

'Why don't you, Alfred,' she said in a voice reminiscent of a spoon scraping the sugar at the bottom of a cup. 'Why don't you,' she stopped, cleared her throat and continued, 'come and have one with me?'

'Naughty girl! You're picking me up. Aren't you? Now be honest. Your cautious ego is running away from you.'

We stood caught in an earthquake of laughter in front of the shop, while people stared and smiled at us.

'Let's get some nice biscuits to dunk,' I suggested.

It was a good walk to her house. Amazing how far some women will walk to save a few pounds. Over coffee she relaxed. I noted her beautifully shaped hands, which ended with long, delicate fingers and well-manicured nails, and I suspect my eyes lingered too obviously over her warm, flowered dress, which barely concealed the bulges which had turned to soft, plushy fat as she over-bloomed. But she was still a handsome woman. I suddenly felt that Jacob McAlpine had served her ill by running off. I wanted to comfort her, to talk about the solitude and anguish of being a widower in search of solace, about my anguish, and compare it with hers – perhaps so similar in texture and content.

Her dog, a snapping glutton for foods unsuitable for dogs, took a violent dislike to anyone who went too close to Lucy. He crunched his biscuits mercilessly, even vengefully, and showed clearly that he objected to my presence.

'Don't worry,' Lucy said consolingly. 'He'll get used to you. He's my little Mutt.' She kissed him noisily and by his attitude he showed that he liked both the sensation and the sound. I discovered, as we talked, how knowledgeable she was about dogs, mink and men. We talked of many things. Many things that held me entranced. She then proceeded to play me a record of some wonderful Dave Brubeck jazz.

'He's my favourite jazz musician. I keep the piano tuned. It's an expensive one. I haven't played it recently.'

'I expect you were very good when you played regularly.'

She went to the piano and began to sing and accompany herself. I could hear longing, sadness, regret. She spoke of Jacob, sullen and moustached, who was, according to her, 'a weak man, a clever but unintelligent man.'

There was a most appetising smell emerging from the kitchen.

'You must be hungry,' she said.

'No, just thirsty.'

'Whatever can a man like you be thirsty for? Something frighteningly sophisticated, I should imagine.'

I went quite close to her and pecked her cheek and whispered, 'Dare me to tell you!'

She looked me full in the face and burst out laughing.

'Alfred, we aren't kids. If you have a menu, let me know what's on offer. I haven't given up on passion.'

'Coffee and dunking biscuits today. We must fortify ourselves for the future.'

'The future?'

She nodded and kissed me suggestively and then passionately. Her dog began to howl as if to reprimand her. We went into her bedroom. Both dogs followed us, jumped on the bed and occupied the middle-ground. We returned to the settee after locking our dogs in the bedroom. The settee was not a comfortable place to be at such a moment of simmering excitement.

'Whatever shall we do?' I joked as we undressed. I sneaked glimpses at her. She had the kind of breasts I had always wanted to touch. Large, bulbous fleshy ones that looked like those in the paintings of the old masters.

'I haven't seen any as beautiful as these,' I said, holding them gently. They were surprisingly heavy. Dear me!

'Aha,' she giggled. 'Then feel free. Here's the floor. Let's do it.' The shock of that remark caused me to resolve never again to judge a book by its cover. Our encounter was a mediocre effort. So many goblins of uncertainty and loss stared at us around every feeling and gesture.

'Better luck next time,' I said and went into her bathroom. The collie snarled at the sound of footsteps it did not recognise. What Sheba was doing I had no idea. Funnily enough, the dogs were always friendly to each other. We humans are just too anxious, I confessed to the man in the mirror.

After Lucy had taken a shower, we ate silently – the soup and bread whose smells had appetised. I was not sure what I could offer her. I felt like a pioneer. I had conquered new territory or, as Finbar put it, answered 'a call to copulation'.

My dog and I departed for home. I wanted quietude to think. My body remembered the strange sea in which I had taken a short spurt. I could not stop thinking about Lucy's exquisite hands moving dextrously over my body, while her manoeuvres reawakened all my dead feelings and memories of missed opportunities. I felt a sharp sense of compulsion to call her. Which I did.

'You're a dear girl, Lucy. Thank you.'

'It's a long time since anyone said that to me. You'd be surprised what I can do with my hands. I could give you a slap for calling me a girl. I am woman, not every woman, mind, just one willing to give chance a chance. What are you doing now?'

'Thinking of our brief encounter.'

'I'm sure we can do better next time.'

'Hang on, Lucy. We're not saplings.'

'I most definitely am in that department. Alas, with many regrets, I am so often disappointed.'

'Come off it, Lucy, a woman of your rarity cannot have, must not have, regrets.'

'A matter of opinion, Alfred. My body does not remember a single loving touch, only moments of pseudo-passion, and conditional love from tacky old men, present company excepted, of course.'

Her voice had become soaked in resentment. I was concerned for her state of mind and blamed myself for pushing her towards an outpouring of unhappy thoughts. I began to try to comfort her, but my door bell rang to the accompaniment of a crying baby. In a rush, I excused myself and ended the conversation.

Declan, Maisie and little Theresa had come to say goodbye. They were going home for a time and would let us know how they were doing. Declan explained that his father now needed help and it was his duty to do his share in the upkeep of the farm. It was amazing to see the independence and intelligence in fussy little Theresa. She held her parents in a noose of over-indulgence. She cried when they picked her up and when they put her down, when they smiled at her and when they didn't. How grateful I was that I had no children to worry about, even as Declan beamed with pride.

'She is my heart, the living image of my sister, Siobhan, except for her eyes which are Maisie's, and when she holds out her arms to me the pride in me is grand,' he confessed, then added, 'But, I come to ask somebody to take care of Ruby, my cat. I would have taken her with us if I hadn't sold the van. I don' want her to run wild. She's a good cat. Do you know anyone?'

'I know who would love a cat. Old Mrs Mack,' I said. She lived two doors from Judy. 'I'll take it to her. Put her down. Sheba loves cats.' I should have said Sheba ignores cats because that's what she did to Ruby, as black as ink with eyes as grey as slate.

'My dad won't give up,' Declan mused. 'He's an old man, but he won't give up, so I know now where I should flick my sweat.'

He wiped his face with the style of an actor of quality and helped his family climb into their battered old car. I watched them drive away without a sliver of doubt that good would follow them home, that they would find peace in the simplicity of village life. I felt a lump in my throat as they left. The baby had been a squirming thing only a short time before, but through her, both parents had begun to feel the need to give up purposeless exile. I watched them go and sat down.

I remembered the story I had read of a man, centuries ago, who fell into a pit late one Friday. His Jewish friends could not rescue him as their Sabbath had begun. The Christians would not rescue him because he was a Jew. In desperation, the man converted to Christianity. But by then it was Sunday and the Christians could not rescue him because it was their day of rest. The Jews would not rescue him because he was a Christian. By Monday the man was dead. I was confused about my own exile. In my heart I was not truly an Englishman; on the evidence of my skin colour and adopted behaviour I was no longer a West Indian. But what did I care? God was in his Heaven taking care of things. Tomorrow was another day and I'd still be an exile.

I went out, took the cat to old Mrs Mack. It was a fine morning and I thought of Lucy again. Like flashes she came into my mind. Like the light of a candle-bug she brightened my moods and then off she went.

It was a few days later when I walked with Sheba in the park and found Uncle Nat in our inner sanctum, still as a stone, except for an outpouring of voice, celebrating the coming of the wallflowers with a prayer. Jamsey Ned was watching him respectfully. There was no Finbar or Judy. I remembered they had told us they going to Birmingham for a week or so.

With raised eyes and uplifted arms, Uncle Nat was saying, 'Thank you, Lord, that I am here in the sun, which you give to all of us with our dark skins, your special blessing to protect us from your heavenly furnace. Let the whiteman make what they like of it, and forgive them their prejudices, but allow us to rail at them, and condemn them, as it is our right so to do.

'Thank you that the hedge in this park, which people try to kill off, is not the mud walls of my grave. Thank you for my eyes to see your handiworks, the birds flying with bits of wood, bits of hair, bits of this and that to make their nests. Help me, Lord, to remember where I put my teeth – I take them out last night and this morning I...'

Suddenly old Mrs Mack came hobbling up as fast as she could, carrying Black Ruby. The cat's eyes were closed, she was limp and covered in paint.

'See,' she sobbed. 'Ruby is nearly dead. They've sprayed her with paint. Some boys done it. What shall I do? Oh, what shall I do?'

Black Ruby was gasping through the fumes, her eyes streaming.

'I knew I would be needed,' said Arabella, arriving at that moment. 'Some force kept on pulling me out of my home and willing me to come here. Telephone the RSPCA! Quick! The paint mustn't dry on the cat. Find someone with a mobile phone. Oh, if only Alana were here.'

The poor cat scratched out and mewed as if it had suddenly become desperate to live.

Judy's voice cut through the commotion. 'Run with her to the pet shop. The vet lives upstairs. Run, Jamsey. Run! Whatever you do, don't drop it!' she shouted from her window.

Everyone was yelling, 'Go, Jamsey! Go, Jamsey!'

The old woman sat sobbing on the grass. 'Why did they do it? They thought it was funny. They laughed. One of them was drunk. The tall lad... I never done him harm!'

'Darwin,' Arabella said out loud. 'That lad is a menace. I've just passed him with thunder on his face.'

'I'll get that tearaway by his long nose,' said Uncle Nat.

'Now, Nathaniel. You were all forgiveness a moment ago,' I said.

CHAPTER NINE

We sat on the benches before realising that they had been repaired and then Arabella gave an enormous shout. A notice had been taped to the Lightning Tree announcing that the Council had agreed that the shed – our haven, shelter and drawing room – should be reconstructed.

'You must read the Bible and tell your troubles to Job, Jonah, Isaiah and Ezekiel and Kings,' Uncle Nat advised.

We applauded the old man's faith and the conviction behind it. Jamsey returned without the cat. The old woman began to weep afresh.

'I had him for twelve years since my Albert went. My son bought him for me before he went to work in Saudi. Now he is gone. I called him Suzy before I realised he was a tom, but he didn't mind what we called him as long as we loved him.'

Grief had confused the old woman. She was talking about her first cat that had died some years before.

'I'll go and have a word with the vet,' I offered. 'It's only six or seven minutes' walk away. Stay here till I get back. I'll be back before you blink.'

As I was about to leave I looked up to see Tiny Dot hurrying by.

'Goodbye,' she called. 'God bless this place if I don't see it again. We have to move on. There's a crowd out there! Some for us! Some against. We have to go.'

We watched her go, wondering how far she'd get before she was moved on again. Her feet seemed unknowing – seeking firm ground but her head was defiantly asserting her contempt for her persecutors.

At the vet's, Alana, now trained as an animal rescue worker, was on duty.

'Is the cat dead?' I asked

'No, far from it. We handle many such cases. We work on birds as well. All that oil, those lead weights and fish hooks! The world is full of evil.'

A man opened the door from the surgery and entered the shop. He was very young, black and bearded, his hair locksed with wax.

'I am Jah Garside.' He was the first vet I ever saw with dreadlocks. He grinned. 'It's my first big challenge. I can't let democracy, history and sensuality die! That's a cat, man! I've cleaned it up. It was not as bad as it looked. Someone tried to wipe off the spray paint and they spread it around. We'll keep Black Ruby for a day or two. Try to get her to drink and then to eat! Cats is us, man! A God in Egypt! We'll send it to the RSPCA Rescue Centre and they'll contact the owner to collect or visit her pet. You can't tell a cat how to be.'

'Thank you, Jah Garside,' I replied gratefully. 'Now for a few words with Mr Darwin.'

'You mean the discoverer of natural selection?'

'A possible descendant of something, Mr Garside, but of what I'm not sure.'

'Call me Jah, man!' he shouted. 'Animals democratise, man!'

He was of a different world. London-born and reared, different from his parents.

When I returned to the park, not a soul was in sight. The park-keeper explained that my posse had gone down to the campsite from which the travellers were to be evicted. To kill boredom, I walked around the park and came upon a large group of people raptly listening to a tall Indian man. In impeccable English he talked about his encounters with the brigands of immigration. He was 'Doc', Rootsman's friend.

Suddenly I caught a glimpse of Lucy through the railings and hurried after her. But she was gone. Was I hallucinating? I returned to Doc's oration but had lost the thread of it.

He was talking with humour and pain about the humiliations he had experienced, and had his audience writhing on the grass with the truths with which he jibed at himself and us who had stayed to endure the hazards of Britain. He was a classic comic, who like Rootsman was illegal, and because he pretended to be someone else, or a visitor on a day trip from 'Chermany', he was not barred from his soapbox. But he had learned survival strategies in our park. He was the first to vanish, as he did that day when the police dropped in.

By now my need for Lucy was overpowering. The others had not returned, so to Lucy's I went. She saw me coming and stood by the door. She did not speak or smile, but she lit up as if a bright band of light had shot through her, changing her colour and making her glow.

'Hello,' I said. 'I need you. Let me show you how much.'

'Do,' she said. 'Please do.' In complete silence we ploughed every depth of desire, said words that were more profound unsaid, and resolved to be together from that moment. It was a marathon that set the tone for all our future intimacies, delights and excursions into the world of flesh-romance. Only much later did I remember Mrs Mack. Heavens! I had to reassure her about the fate of her cat! I snapped into my clothes and was soon on my way.

Mrs Mack had given up hope of ever seeing her cat alive again, and was ecstatic over my good news. Returning home later, I was still boiling with leftover energy! I cleaned my little cottage. A glance at the garden made my heart sink. It was like a desert, but then there were the flowers in the park to cheer me on to summer. I blanked the unkempt garden from my mind and made myself a coffee. Only Lucy mattered. As I sipped the coffee and relived my last moments with the woman who had satisfied me utterly, Arabella returned with Honey and Sheba. She had thunder in her eyes. They looked smudged rather than clean blue.

'Those four-cornered bastards! Those landowners hunted the travellers off their land, while smug council official wimps in suits stood there gloating,' she hissed. 'I was so angry I threw Honey's sausages at them. They need to have their buttocks roasted over raging flames...'

'Really, Arabella, that would be a clear case of savagery.'

'I don't care what it is. They would have got what they deserve.'

'You're in fine form today.'

'We went to the vet's, to meet up with you and an interesting young man explained all to me. His hair is really splendid. Mrs Mack's cat will be fine,' Arabella explained.

I nodded that I knew. 'Would you like tea?'

'Yes, Earl Grey if at all possible.'

I made plain ordinary tea (Typhoo, I think), put out some biscuits and sat down. Nothing like a cup of tea to cement feelings of likeability, especially for Arabella. She always took me back to a time, probably mythical, when manners meant everything. She sipped her tea with great delicacy.

'Wonderful aroma, Earl Grey,' she said, wiping her lips, with great delicacy. 'Have you got a whisky as well? I need one.'

'You can differentiate teas?'

'It's my nose, my dear. Better than Honey's.'

I wanted to tell her that her nose and taste had failed her but didn't.

We offered the dogs some plain biscuits. They declined. They preferred the chocolate-coated kind.

'Another thing, Alfred,' Arabella said. 'I have a request to make.'

'Go on, and no histrionics, Arabella.'

'Would you come, please, would you come with me to the oldies' tea-dance, day after tomorrow?'

'Oldies' tea-dance? Never heard of it!'

'It's a monthly event. I haven't been for months. I needed

a partner since Harold hopped it.'

'Get him back!' I said. 'And quick! I'm no dancer. Find a partner there.'

'Don't get me wrong. There are men there, some married, with wives who behave territorially. There are also not-marrieds and widowers, but they are seized upon by the many not so young and lovely Harpies waiting to grab them.'

'I won't believe you if you say you're not in the pack, Arabella. You've never scored a duck with men, have you?'

'Not when I play my mature judgements. With Harold it was all naïve instinct and vital curiosity – the teenager's disease.'

She laughed and then added seriously, 'You must come! Lucy has been so helpful. The quartet had no pianist and she agreed to attend as piano player provided they stuck to the old tunes we all know so well.'

CHAPTER TEN

During the day of the dance I thought little about being present at a gathering of terpsichorean dinosaurs, but my nerves began to prick and shout as the hour approached. I recalled Arabella's stern, 'Three o'clock sharp! And whatever you do, don't saunter in! Stride in, Alfred.'

But what should I wear for striding in? A riding outfit? Should I be formal or informal? I couldn't imagine! I decided to please myself and wear light, formal clothes. If I overheated I'd escape from my tie. But just so I should not disgrace myself, I rang Arabella to confirm my outfit.

'Surely you know what to wear, Alfred! Be adventurous! Come in your birthday suit! The devil will find a lot for our idle hands to do – and to music!' I hung up the telephone to cut off her laughter.

Hopefully suitably clad, I made my way to the Horse and Hounds pub, at the back of which were some private rooms. I heard laughter and posh accents as I drew nearer. Arabella was certainly present, and this was definitely, from sound alone, the kind of company one strode into.

'Ah, there you are!' she said, as she came towards me. She took my arm and wove me through the gathering. I was duly introduced to 'everyone' and then had a glass of champagne pushed into my hand.

'They're a fine bunch,' whispered Arabella. 'Mostly retired theatre and other professions. All keen as steel to dance. They make me proud of my profession. They speak admirably – their voices so engaging and pleasantly refined.'

'Nonsense! They all have very keen, piercing voices, to my ears. Why drag me among them?'

'Don't fuss so.'

'Where's Lucy?'

'Exploring the piano. It's so energising to dance to real music.'

Lucy avoided my eyes, but I went over and chatted briefly to her. Each time I saw her, I noticed something freshly endearing about her. Her voice didn't show insecurity, but self-control. She behaved calmly; was it simply the fear of leaping into things? I began to think of her as interesting, wise and lovable. I surveyed the room and took in the decor designed for ambience rather than comfort. The room was long and wide, allowing for tables to be arranged for groups of five. Ten tables in all for about fifty people. There was an open space for dancing and just a few yards away sat the quartet. They tuned up. As well as Lucy on the piano, there was a saxophone, violin and bass.

'Ah, a saxophonist. I like the saxophone,' I said. While we fixed our carnations and seated ourselves, the saxophonist played a mournful, dirgelike version of 'Autumn Leaves'.

'Well done, old chap,' called Nelson, an army man. 'But no need to rub it in!'

They jazzed it up a bit after that, and couples danced a kind of speeded up sleep-walking. Everyone cheered. We continued through waltzes, quicksteps, two-steps, tangos and sambas until the national anthem, for which we all stood up, was played.

I went over to Lucy, 'You must be tired. Can I help?'

'Yes please. You could buy me a drink in the pub in ten minutes or so.'

Arabella patted me on the shoulder. 'This is just a temporary arrangement, Alfred. I told you Harold flunked it. But he'll be back.'

Lucy and I sat in the pub. Lucy was quiet and we hardly spoke. I wondered whether it was just that she was tired, or whether she wanted to cool matters a little. I felt so much at ease with her, but wondered whether I could still be a seriously sexual creature at my age. Judy I saw as a one-off event and I didn't really belong to Arabella's world with its faded charm and revival of froth. I walked Lucy home.

'I'm tired. I'll have a bath and then to bed. We've said all we needed to say today. We must think about our dogs, Alfred.'

'Yes, Sheba will be patiently awaiting my return,' I hurriedly agreed.

The outing to the tea-dance had been an enjoyable one but whether I would repeat it remained to be seen.

For the next week or so I gave attention mainly to my dog and her concerns. Her injections were due, and she needed to have her nails trimmed, her ears examined and her coat groomed. Alana would come. A good girl, Alana, no longer the drama queen of the pet shop. One could get her to groom dogs at home, which she often did. On summer days she gave puppet-shows to teach pet-care to young children in the nearby nursery schools. She had become an indefatigable asset to our community. A care-giver in the making, perhaps to be like Judy one day. Actually I was beginning to miss Judy and Finbar since their jaunt to attend some fine function in Birmingham. There was so much to talk about.

Spring changed to early summer. When the sun shone, everything looked gold-tinted. I wandered into the park and to my utmost delight Barker ran up to me.

'Barker!' I cried. 'You're back. Where's your dad?'

'Don't be so daft. I'm not the creature's dad. He's my dog. I'm his master and friend.' There was Finbar.

'Well,' I said. 'Long time no see.'

'A fortnight, that's all.'

'You were truly missed.' I told him about the cat and our suspicions of Darwin's involvement in the paint-spraying, and his disappearance.'

'Darwin's around,' Finbar said. 'He told me some confused story about a cat and how you all thought he had harmed it. He swore on his mother's bunions it wasn't him. But I'll be keeping an eye on him. He was dropping in at Judy's before we went away, and she is ready to start mothering him. He came over to my place as well. Unhealthily fascinated he was with my brother Phelim's air-gun. I keep it as a memento. Darwin always wants to hold it and asks hundreds of questions about it.'

With Finbar's return every aspect of our park had fallen into place. Seamus once more made tea. Jamsey fussed the dogs. Judy waved from her window. The familiar had returned. We talked of having a dog show to collect funds for the homeless, but decided that dog shows were too owner-driven. When next we saw Arabella we put the idea to her.

She scratched her head, gave a histrionic pout, fell into the character of perplexed governess and finally spoke.

'Excellent idea but not feasible. We won't have enough dogs. But why don't we have a "bone-hunt" with the dogs? We played that scores of times in my youth. Great fun!'

'Bone-hunt, Arabella? I've never heard of it but if you say...'

'Certainly. We could hide a variety of cooked bones in our part of the park and set the dogs to find them. The dog who is greedy enough to find more than one would be the winner.'

I thought that was attributing to the dogs the ability to reason, but it was not for me to disagree with Arabella, especially when supported by Finbar, Judy and Jamsey. I told Lucy about our plan over the telephone. She wanted no part of it and excluded her collie Mutt, although she confided that he was by far and away cleverer than Honey.

The weather being fine, we bought a selection of boiled sheep, cow and calf bones; and although the flies hovered over the clingfilm encasing them, we were hopeful that the dogs would respond to our command, 'Seek! Seek! Seek!'

We brought brightly coloured bows for our dogs. Honey looked resplendent in red, Sheba in sober blue, Barker in green, Lyds in yellow, Alana's dog, Robbie, in purple and Declan's deserted dog, Browse, in brown to match his coat. A crowd came to watch. Before we sent them off to find the bones, we gave the scent to each one, replaced the bones in their various hiding places and paraded the dogs before a small crowd of usually housebound pensioners, hobbling out for the day. Some sang old songs and recited for us, quite why, no one knew.

Then we set the dogs on the trail of bones. Barker and Sheba at once understood. I had not fed Sheba so she needed food. The others, ignoring their owners' commands, started to gambol on the grass. Robby, renegade stud that he was, tried his luck with any bitch he could get under his back legs, in spite of his smart plaid pants and sunglasses.

'Alana,' growled Finbar. 'What's up with that sexploitative insect you call a dog? Tell him to keep his zip done up. He's so hot!'

She swept up her dog and went off in a huff. A wild-eyed Dalmatian had wandered in and lost no time growling and snarling for a share. A fierce fight began. Other dogs rushed in. Sheba with snarls and growls sat protecting her bone from Honey. Arabella stooped beside both dogs, urging Honey to let Sheba have the bone she'd found.

'It's smelly, darling, and don't be a dog in the manger! Let her have the bellyache.'

Just then there was the sound of shots. People ran in all directions. Arabella threw herself over my dog and hers to protect them.

Barker took a shot in his chest and lay on the grass whimpering. His blood, a red line, his bow undone. I looked in the direction of the noise. Darwin walked purposefully across the same green grass, firing an air rifle as he proceeded, turning it on every dog silly enough to stay in range. His glazed-over eyes showed his fiery anger. He yelled his hatred of dogs and their owners – people like us who pampered their dogs, who did not care if he ate poison.

'Show me where they are! Let me kill them!' he shouted. Finbar grabbed him from behind and held him down. Darwin swore like a family of hooligans in his alcoholic fog, and screamed the dreaming of his demons. People ran towards the dogs. I pulled Arabella to her feet. Alana, carrying Robby, called for help from the police on her mobile phone, and then urged Jah Garside to come at once with the pet ambulance.

'It's mayhem here. May-bloody-hem!' she yelled.

Soon afterwards Darwin, now pinned down, had come to his senses and cried, 'I want my Ma! Get my Ma for me!'

'Shut up!' said Finbar. 'You've killed my dog. You've killed him! I can't believe it. He was so intelligent. He was so happy. I have had him for many years, eight years! I can't believe he's gone. Oh God, take him to heaven!' Finbar wept with loss and love.

'He may not die,' I said. 'Jah Garside will be with him any moment now.'

Finbar was in a dreadful state. 'Barker's been everything to me! He saved my life when I was lost and down. He was everything to me!' he sobbed.

Judy came towards us. She said nothing but her eyes were full of tears. Barker had indeed been shot to death.

By now the police had arrived and were struggling with Darwin. Finbar, sobbing and pleading with Barker to wag his tail, carried him to the ambulance. Alana asked no one in particular how any one could be so monstrous as to kill a dog. The pensioners looked confused.

'I have lived through two wars and this is just as bad – killing innocence like this,' said one old man. 'They didn't hurt no one. The poor creature took the shot in his chest.'

The dogs not hurt slunk away and hid whimpering even at their shadows. As well as the fatal shot to Barker, Judy's Lyds had been wounded, as had the wild-eyed Dalmation.

Finbar recovered his composure and gave his orders. 'Alana, I want him buried. Dress him well. Red trousers, plaid coat, red bow tie and plaid shoes. I want roses in his coffin. He was my friend. He was everything to me. I'll pay whatever it costs.'

I put my arm around Finbar, now looking old and drained, and led him across the park to my home. Arabella followed, still clutching Honey.

Jamsey carried Sheba.

'Heavens!' said Arabella. 'This is beyond belief. One minute all is quiet. The next minute it's mayhem! I need a stiff drink. We all do.'

Finbar downed his whisky, his lips quivering, his voice dark and heavy and blistered by shock. The dam of grief burst in his heart. Face buried in the palms of his hands, he sobbed Barker's name more than a dozen times.

'Talk about him!' said Arabella. 'He obviously meant more than most to you.'

Finbar shook his head and dried away his tears. 'It's a long story,' he said. 'But I need to start at the beginning, back home in Ireland, if you're going to understand what Barker meant to me.

'We were a large and loving family – three girls and two boys, me and Phelim, my older brother, whom I followed everywhere. We worked a small farm but Pa had a trade. He was a carpenter, and Phelim, a handsome young lad, was going to follow Pa's trade. He was a daredevil. No fear in any part of him. No path too dark. No hill too high for him to climb. No sea too rough to swim. He was my hero. He taught me to swim, to fiddle, to use Pa's tools and put them all back where they should be or take the consequence. One day he went climbing with some lads his own age. Sadly he fell from a cliff onto a ridge a little way down. He lay there hurt. He tried to get up and rolled over to right himself, but he fell into the sea. He was drowned. Only God saw him die. It destroyed my Ma. "I never said goodbye to him," she

85

sobbed. "I never thought he wouldn't come home again. The sea took my son from me."

'I loved Sundays. First we went to mass and then to the cemetery where we spent time with my brother. After a while Ma was able to accept that God had wanted my brother with Him. She also said I would please him and all my family by becoming a priest. I was happy and Father O'Hanley took over my education. He was old, wise and clever and taught us boys about the Church. I grew into a happy boy, eager to serve as a chorister and altar boy. I loved the services. My Pa watched me with pride and talked of my future with hope. My two older sisters, only a year apart, got married to two chaps who had come home from America for a smell of the air. They had grand weddings, and as Phelim was not there for the fiddling, I took his fiddle and surprised myself with it.

'The girls loved the fiddling! It was just as if Phelim, the Lord of the Fiddle, had come alive in my bow-arm. I felt the music moving in me, tumultuous and then calm. I could taste the sugar of the melody coming out in my sweat. After that, my fight to resist girls began. I loved the Church, but slowly I began to love girls. I read the lives of the saints, travelled with them through every temptation, but the eyes of beauteous girls rested upon me, and I began to sneak smiles at them in between my prayers.

'To walk away from them, I took to the fields in contemplation of my future, and then one day I met my fate in a girl called Benedicta. Everybody loved her. She made you thank God that you had eyes to see such a sight as she walking in the fields, looking at the water or picking cress from the stream. Some said she had a wicked side to her, a side which made her a tease for the lads such as meself.

'All summer I wandered around the country playing my fiddle at weddings. Oh the shame of it! The drinking got worse and I continued to love girls, write poetry about them, and when life grew dark I walked naked through the nettles as a penitent. The guilt was struggling in me. I prayed to be pure and they called me Mr Pious.

'One day I sat on a little mound. The sun was bright and clean. Birds were dashing in and out of the sea, fishing and flying across the wide blue, while others cawed and cooed with the delight of living. I walked round the hillock and a pair of strong hands seized me, and pulled me out of sight into its shadow side. I looked around hoping to see my brother's ghost, but instead there was Benedicta's seductive form – smooth skin, tight apple-sized tits, backside worthy of a pinch or two.

'"Why are you acting all holy, Finbar Macgwin? Don't you know what lips are for, hands are for and that big dickie there, raising himself at the touch of my hand, like that of the giant Finn McCool?" She soon had me down. In next to no time I was out of my clothes, the sprigs of grass under my back and me covering myself from the gaze of a determined woman. She smiled and said, "Now there's a bed of roses beneath you, a jig or two or three won't hurt you. Fiddle with me!" We spent a good few hours coming and going, rolling and tumbling on that sweet grass, with us fighting to become the best fiddlers of that particular day.

'Thoughts of the Church were beginning to blur. My one lust was for life. The girls continued to dance like dervishes to my fiddle. Pa and Ma lost hope in me and there was so much argument that I crossed the water to get away from Benedicta, whose loving puppy I had become, and then there was Bernie who insisted, her voice as persistent as a pneumatic drill, after I'd done no more than kissed her, that I must marry her.

'So to England I came and took rooms with other foreign people in Notting Hill. It was a bad time for us. The racists often prevented some of us from going to work, and those at work from coming home.

'I hit the drink while fiddling round the pubs in North London. Drink prevented me from feeling guilty at leaving my old mother, and the grave of my only brother to be tended by my old father. I lost touch with my family and was always drunk – older than Darwin, but always drunk. This went on for years and years.

'One day I wandered down to Chelsea wharf and thinking I could walk on water, I walked fully dressed into the river. I couldn't believe it. I started first to pray and then to swim. I shouted for help. No one was about the river on that dark night. Only lights dancing in the distance. I shouted again and then I felt something grip me. It began pulling me towards the bank. It was a dog. I grabbed the rope of a buoy moored close by. I shouted for help again. Then a man and a woman pulled me out. "Nothing is worth killing yourself over," said the woman.

'"He's drunk," said the man. "Call the police."

'They came and took me to sleep it off in the police cells and set me free next morning. I went straight to the local church and the priest helped me. I have the occasional glass of whisky but I never again got drunk since then. I walked down to the river several days later and stood close to the spot where I nearly drowned that fateful night, and five minutes later the dog, the same dog, appeared wagging its tail. He lived on his own by the river, surviving as best he could. He belonged to himself. He had a strong bark. I called him Barker. Eight years later he was murdered.'

Finbar broke down again. We were all in tears, even Arabella.

'I know that feeling of loss,' she said. 'It's like a deep cut. A clean cut from which pain floods out and touches every other part of living. Poor Barker! A noble death!'

'What will they do to Darwin? Slap his wrist and say, "Naughty boy"?'

'No,' said Finbar. 'He killed my dog. He will receive his just desserts. Forget him.'

There was vengeance and resolution in Finbar's voice. We were so involved with his loss, that for a day or so Judy slipped into the shadows of our minds. Her Lyds who had taken shots in the face, had been taken to the hospital in Victoria, a private hospital where a dog got what its owner could afford. That was all I knew. Later that day I made a special effort to get down there. Judy, looking sad and pale, was in the waiting room alone. The cup of tea which the nurses had given her sat untouched on a small table beside her. I went to find a nurse and asked to see poor Lyds. She was lying in a large comfortable cage with a drip attached to her, in the intensive care unit.

The vet peered at her and then said, 'It isn't as bad as it looks.'

'Lyds,' I said. 'How are you, old girl?' Her ear moved.

'She can hear you. She took a shot in the eye, but there will only be minimal loss of sight. As she ages, well, who knows?'

'Does the owner know?'

'Of course. We tell the truth here.'

'May I stroke her gently?'

He nodded. As I stroked her she took a deep breath, her leg moved and she lay still again.

'She has been heavily sedated,' the vet whispered. 'She would have been in serious pain when we tried to remove the shots. It was a vicious attack. I'd like to do it back to him. At least he could shield his face with his hands.'

I returned to Judy, who asked, 'Do you think she'll be all right?'

'The vet says she will be. Says she's not in pain now.'

'Do you ever fancy me, Alfred?' Judy asked.

'I did one time.'

She patted my hand. 'I can't tell what I'd do without Lyds. She has never been unfaithful to me, spurned me or used me.'

'You're a wonderful friend, Judy. I cherish the memory.'

CHAPTER ELEVEN

I'd never known Judy to be silent, but on the way home she was. She knew Barker was lying in his glass-covered coffin at the back room of the pet shop.

When he was loaded onto a van by Finbar and Jamsey, to be taken away to a pet cemetery outside London, crowds of people silently watched. Then they began to shout:

'God keep you safe!'. 'In his heaven'. 'We'll all miss you'. 'More than you'll ever know'. 'You were very bold and clever'. 'There is no other quite like you'. 'God keep you'. 'We will remember you.' Clichés from start to finish, but serious clichés, boiled up on the spot!

There was a single wreath made of flowers from the park. It said 'From park people and friends'.

Later, the ordeal of parting over, the park seemed empty without the two dogs. The papers had heard of the tragedy and trumpeted: 'LAD RAMPANT WITH ECSTASY', 'DRUG-CRAZED HOOLIGAN TAKES GUN TO PET'S PEEPERS' and 'BARKER BARKS NO MORE'. Donations were solicited for the RSPCA to fight cruel 'savages' who, one writer to the paper asserted, should be 'encouraged to murder themselves'.

The stories were inaccurate and annoying, but we let the whole nonsense pass without comment. One even claimed that the intended victim was Uncle Nat, who was supposed to be thanking God because he had been spared. He had called on his 'African God' with the sound of every shot and his God had come to his aid – so one of the daily rags informed the nation. Another told how a 'dog-show' arranged by a mature actress, Arabella Biggin-Heyho, had been ruined by a drug-crazed youth with a grudge against anti-vivisectionists and the 'decent dog-loving British public'. Hoards of journalists appeared in the park hunting down anything that resembled a story, true or false.

'Let's desert the park,' Arabella suggested. 'All this is too much.'

We agreed entirely and, incandescent with anger, kept out of the park. Such visitors 'made us sick'. Finbar decided to go home and ascertain the fate of his two loves, Bernie and Benedicta. Barkatoo, his new gift-pup would go with him. London, indeed our park, had lost its appeal.

Alana decided to train as an RSPCA inspector, two or three rungs further up than an animal rescue worker.

'It's long and hard,' we warned her, but she was determined to broaden her experience and enter the dog-professional world.

'I'll still help you lot if I can,' she promised. 'I prefer animals to people, as you well know. And that's the truth. And I'm not ashamed to say it. I like only a very few people.'

'What will become of the pet-shop?' I asked.

'It's being swallowed up. Taken over by Anaconda and Company. They offered me a job at £2 an hour, part-time. I'd end up begging in the street. Three days at £10 a day! Huh! Signing-on for help is not for me.'

We returned to our various concerns, all of us pampering Lyds during her recovery. Our resolution to keep out of the park did not last for long. The reporters, who had proliferated like maggots and pontificated like priests, went away, the weather was good and we felt that we owed it to Lyds to help her get over her aversion to the park, which at first she shied away from. But, after seeing an animal behaviourist, she made some progress, and after longer and longer periods of exposure, she returned to play with Sheba, Honey, the deaf Doberman, and Finbar's new Barkatoo – before he accompanied his master back home. Jamsey had found one of Barker's sons, and that was a comfort to all who loved Barker. Finbar decided to mate him with a bitch he was negotiating to purchase. We wished him luck.

Summer was passing fast. Only Judy had not come back to the park, which she still felt distrustful of. Yet she still gave destitute people tea and helped and advised the youth. But if she knew where Darwin was, or had any news of his whereabouts, she told no one.

Our park became a tourist stop. Coaches parked close by and decanted eager men and women festooned with cameras and wearing designer t-shirts that read, 'Barker still Barks', or 'Barker Barks No More!' or 'Where is Darwin? I want his Nuts'. Some t-shirts were decorated with a spot of blood on very green grass, and a variety of captions: 'He fell here. He fell there'. 'The noble creature peed here'. 'It happened here'. 'Death Happens', and 'Hilburnel Park'. We all had photographs taken with visitors, near the spot where Barker fell. Fresh bunches of flowers appeared. Teddy bears and other toys mushroomed on different spots – what people called the 'Scene of the Event'.

One day Arabella and Harold, who had finally reappeared, came to tea. I asked Judy over but Lyds still hated being left. She howled when Judy went out and wasn't even able to be left with friends.

'Oh, you can be sure that some do-gooder will telephone the RSPCA to say a dog is being neglected. Sorry, later in the week, perhaps,' Judy said peevishly.

'We came to talk about the club. Hope you don't mind,' Arabella began in a sugary tone.

'Yes, we hope you don't,' added Harold.

'Club?' I asked through a fog of incomprehension. 'What club?'

'The tea-dance club? Surely you remember!'

'You mean the oldies' thingamajig? What's there to talk about? Harold's back! And he'll be much more a dancer than I ever was. He knows all the turns.'

'It's not the *turns*, Alfred. Don't be such a pleb. Harold knows the *steps*. But we'd still like you to come. There are always available spinsters, widows and others willing to dance with any unattached man.'

'Sure, I'll come.'

They drank several cups of tea, liberally helped themselves to my biscuits, then to fruit and started to leave with smiles of satisfaction on their faces.

'Be careful, Harold. You have a banana in your pocket. Mind how you sit down.'

He took it out and handed it to Arabella who promptly ate it. I watched them, all the while wondering what it was that bound them so firmly together. Arm in arm they walked, heart to heart and eye to eye, like two people who, despite all their prevarications and disavowals, were cemented by some strange process of loving and belonging.

With Finbar away, and the others dispersed, life became dull, but I would not allow myself to be bored. I worked in my garden, walked on the Heath, which sometimes made a change from the park, and spent much time with Judy, helping her to talk out the horror of the attack on the dogs.

Once in a while Lucy came too and then we went home to our garden of delights. She was now and then working part-time, selling 'Whole Life Vitamins' for a continental firm. She found the work frustrating, since the people whom she was convinced needed the vitamins could not afford to buy them.

'I'm tired of lying to young people,' she said. 'What they need is sensible food. They can't afford books, fees *and* food. They have to borrow or cadge. The policy-makers have fostered a cult of thievery and dishonesty. I'm giving up this pick-pocketing to volunteer at a home for the elderly, a hospital, or some place else.'

'You need cheering up. Let's go together to the tea-dance. Arabella is paired up with her darling Harold. He's back.'

Lucy's smile was wide and full of meaning.

'You mean the tea-dance at which I played? OK. I'll dance to someone else's music, this time!'

For the first time since the shootings, I felt the turbulence of expectation and excitement. In retrospect, my first oldie dance had been an amusing afternoon.

CHAPTER TWELVE

It rained on the morning of the tea-dance, but by the time I called for Lucy the sun was glowing and a gentle breeze tempered the heat.

'How do I look? Just to annoy Arabella I bought something with spots on. She hates spots.' Lucy laughed mischievously.

'You look "fab", as the youth would once say. I say you look prosperous.' I didn't dare add that spots made her look substantial.

I wore the light suit of my previous visit. I'm sure I looked affluent and polished. When we entered the room it seemed smaller. There were more chairs and more people. I heard Arabella before I saw her. Harold carried Honey. They had even brought her basket so that she could be comfortable when they danced.

'Hello, hon,' I said. 'Hello, you two.'

'Not so loud, Alfred. Remember her trauma.'

'Give her a kick in the behind and untraumatise that emaciated spectre,' said Lucy. 'I think that dog needs to be kicked. It's so spoilt, so sour, so dreadfully bratty.'

Arabella, collecting her venom, pretended to ignore Lucy.

'Ah,' she said at last. 'Lucy. I was trying to work out who it was in yellow with brown leopard spots and that coarse growl.'

'Thank you, Arabella. I'm so pleased you saved cheetah for yourself.'

The band struck up a tango. Arabella delicately placed Honey in her basket.

'Shall we, my dear?' chortled Harold.

'Of course.'

They danced a veritable tango exhibition. The chattering classes, ever ready with their opinions, clapped, said, 'Marvellous! How divine! Pure essence! 'Bravissimo.'

Arabella curtsied. Honey climbed out of her basket and, wiggling her tail, sat under the food table.

'By the way,' said Simon the ex-official. 'I heard about that fracas in the park. What became of the bounder who killed all those dogs?'

'It was only one,' I informed him.

'One or six, what does it matter? He should have been horsewhipped.'

'Bring back the stocks, I say,' his wife piped in her thin string of a voice.

'No, put a hole in his behind with the tip of a boot. That would teach the rat to kill dogs.'

'That was just too terrible! Fancy killing dogs when there are so many undesirables about.'

'And the government is not keeping its end up! All the taxes we pay and we're still short of jails!'

'Don't fib, John. You have a clever accountant. You don't pay out much in tax.'

'True, but I don't get off scot-free.'

Lucy looked at me. There was disgust all over her face at what was being said.

'Have they found the culprit?'

'Yes,' said Lucy. 'They hanged him, and then dragged him round the park till he disintegrated – like they did in olden days.'

'Really?' said a chorus of voices.

'We missed it. Served the bounder right.'

We edged out of the company.

'Can you believe it, Lucy? Is it callousness or stupidity?'

'It's neither. It's their code. They use it to conceal their true feelings. It's simply a manner of speaking.'

'Do you want to leave?'

'You must be joking. I won't let this tribe of ancient perverts prevent me enjoying myself.'

We danced. Waltzes, quick-steps, tangos. We were well pleased with ourselves. It was nearly ten o'clock when I walked Lucy home.

We went indoors, sat down and had a large gin and tonic. It put her in a girlish, giggling mood.

'Alfred,' she said. 'Excuse me for a minute, but when I say "Oo-hoo! Come and get it!" Come into my maison deluxe.'

I did as she asked.

'Well, Alfred,' she said. 'Here I am in my birthday suit. Now get into yours.'

Once more my ego and I rose to the occasion, penetrating the accretions of time, mimicking youth. Time flashed past but I was conscious of having had a second very good feast. The dogs ran in and looked at us as if asking what were we up to. I felt a little ashamed. What if Sheba understood?

My perceptions were sharper as I walked home. A full moon roamed the skies. I was on top of the world. Lucy had been a really delicious partner, unselfish, co-operative and truly generous. As I approached my home I noticed a shadow. A man's shadow. The spectre of mugging froze my poor befuddled brain. I carried a mere ten pounds – barely enough for a wrap of heroin, or any of the current designer drugs. My heart began to drum against my breast. I was weak with fear. Too close to run, I saw in my mind those fish floating belly-up in the pond after Darwin and his friends had tipped drugs into the fish pond to fox the police.

'Hello, Sheba! Hello, Mr Alfred!'

Sheba ran to the voice and jumped up.

'Darwin!' I yelled. 'Where have you come from?'

'Please, Mr Alfred, I came back. Finbar will hurt me and his friends will hurt me too.'

'So why have you come back?'

'It's like living with death in that place. Everybody has

gone. I was only there with me Ma, and my brother who wants to beat the shit out of me. He thinks he is me dad. His wife won't leave me alone. She fancies me, so I ran. Please let me stay in your place tonight.'

'Darwin, you're right. You will be given the treatment and you deserve it. Besides, you put the frighteners on me. Fancy coming out of the shadows like that.'

'I am so tired. The bridge is no place to crawl under.'

'All right. Come in! Come in!'

He was in a pitiable state. Like a chicken that had fallen into a muddy pond. My heart bled for him. I offered him a shower and clean clothes, the trousers a little short in the leg. I offered him a bed. In the morning I took him out to buy some jeans he could call his own. His old clothes smelt like a sewer. I forbade him to leave the house while I visited Judy to ask what could be done to save him from his folly.

Jah Garside, who was on his monthly visit to Lyds, was sipping a cup of tea, so I had time to sit down and turn over my thoughts.

After Jah had gone, I told her that Darwin had returned.

'Heavens above! You mean he's here! Those boys who are out for revenge for that Dalmation – they're tearaways. They'll have his hide. I'll go and see them and try and pacify them. Leave it with me for a day or two. I'll come and collect him later.'

The day seemed as long as coils of rope. At last I heard Judy call out.

'Come on, Darwin! Heft yourself out here.' I was determined to contribute nothing.

He began to do his youngest-child act. Sobbing and crying, and saying that he didn't mean it. He didn't know the dogs were there; he didn't know the gun could fire at dogs. He didn't tell the gun to do anything.

'You have to go back to college.'

He shook his head.

'I'm going to get a job and pay my debts and do good.'

'We're going to make sure that you do,' we both said together. 'You were given six months' Community Service in an old people's home by the court. We are going to make sure you do it.' We did so by marching him along to his probation officer and so to his duties at Webb House. It was a pleasure to set him to work on the Tuesday.

It rained all day on Wednesday but on Thursday I woke up to golden sunshine, and to eager anticipation of further entertainments with Lucy. We talked on the phone and agreed that we had the mental set for dancing. Lucy also said she'd tell me more about her researches into her ancestors, the Thistlewoods. When we'd last been in the pub she'd mentioned that she was doing this research. I'd gathered that the Thistlewoods were Jamaican plantation owners in the eighteenth century. At the time I'd said nothing, though a little palpitation passed through my heart. I'd grown so accustomed to saying nothing about my background. Maybe Lucy was the one with whom I'd share it.

Time passed quickly and the day of our third tea-dance rapidly approached. I went round to deposit my dog in the company of Mutt, before setting off with Lucy.

There was a healthy gathering when we arrived. A cluster of colourful clothes revealed legs and arms that had been only mildly touched by sunlight, reminding me of the pallor of those fish that live deep under the sea.

Everyone greeted us warmly. 'I say! Are you two an item?' called inquisitive Ben Festus.

'Yes,' I replied. 'An innocuous, over-the-hill item.'

'More than that, I should think. If not, you ought to be,' his wife Martha added. 'After all, what is life for, but to have a nice man like Alfred stroking your hair?'

It was then I noticed a sedate, half-hidden person in a long, frilly, off-white skirt and a short-sleeved red top. No need to guess if she was angry. There was thunder and lightning all over her face. Her eyes were glued to the door.

'Arabella! Fancy hiding away like that!'

'Hello, you two. Hello,' she snapped without taking her eyes off the door. Swiftly she turned to me and blurted out:

'Have you seen Harold? Have you seen that asterisk asterisk asterisk asterisk?' Then, her voice falling into doleful cadences, she added, 'I do so want him to come.'

'He'll come soon,' consoled Lucy. 'He won't let you down.'

We moved to the bar. Arabella looked as if she had never smiled in her life. She walked around the tables saying how dusty they were. They were clustered too closely together, leaving too little space to move. The club had suddenly become oppressive, full to the brim with Philistines and end-of-the-pier blackguards, reflecting the shady world in which some of our number moved.

Then Harold, wearing white trousers, a dark red silk jacket and a smart Panama hat, walked in with a most spectacular young woman on his arm. The silence fell like dust over the crowd and overflowed into a crash of coins from Arabella's purse, running all over the floor to be chased by Honey. She had fled Arabella's embrace to greet Harold.

'Wow,' whispered Lucy. 'What a to-do. What a creature!'

Permed orange hair, powdered face, lips outlined in black with bright orange lipstick, black nail polish, and a bottom-hugging white skirt with matching T-shirt emblazoned with 'I'm all of that! Watch it!'

Arabella was shocked into a conflagration. She was as red as a strawberry. Lucy went over and touched her arm.

'I'm OK, Lucy. I'm angry but I won't ignite.'

She gulped. The tango struck up. She held out her hands in anticipation, but Harold had thrown himself into a very storm of a tango with his companion. Everyone left the floor to them.

'Get her, Honey!' Arabella ordered. Honey obeyed, but ignored the young woman and clung to Harold's leg, causing a hurricane of laughter to erupt.

'You will be decapitated if you hurt Honey, Harold! I mean it!' Arabella yelled.

It seemed like an eternity before there was a hesitant, slight patter of applause. 'Not half as good! Arabella never fumbles! Clean steps all the way!'

Harold bowed and said, 'My new partner for the eternal tango! Felicia Samuel.' Before anyone could reply, he waved an airy hand to Arabella and called over to her.

'How are you, old girl! How are you? I told Felicia about your power over the tango... I honestly didn't see you over there.'

She was stung by Harold's betrayal – in front of her friends.

She staggered to the bar. 'I want a drink,' she said. 'A whisky! Double! Neat!'

Rapidly the young bartender poured the drink, but her hand slipped slowly away from it and she fell to the floor. Releasing Felicia as if she had become an unbearable flame, Harold rushed over to Arabella, tenderly gathered her dancing skirt of net and taffeta about her, and lifted her to a chair. He knelt beside her. Arabella moaned dramatically, her head sagging, the blonde wig asserting itself.

'Where am I?' She mouthed in gossamer-like whispers.

'Here, old girl, beside me. In every corner of my heart,' Harold soothed.

Honey ran round the other side, struggled up into her lap and licked her face. Arabella did one of her swoons. Was it a fake this time? Honey whined. Dogs can smell psychic pain.

'Where am I?' Arabella breathed again. 'Horror of horrors, I am unloved. My pride is being torn to shreds.'

We surrounded her.

'Oh my darling,' wept Harold. 'My only true love,' he sobbed. 'It was nothing; just the passion of the tango. I danced every step with you.' He prolonged the 'you' an extra beat or two.

Arabella wriggled a little and closed her eyes with a sigh.

'Help me up, please, someone. Anyone but you, Harold. You are nothing but a fake, full of subterfuges! You are a phillumenist!'

'What's that?' growled Lucy, fed up to the teeth with the drama.

'A collector of matchbox labels,' Arabella explained wearily. 'Soiled ones.'

Felicia moved towards Harold. 'You know wot I fink? I fink you an' bloody 'er is Laurel an' Hardy's grandmuvver in drag. You don' seriously fink I wanna dance wiv you?' When she reached the door she called out in an even more oiky voice, 'Oy, Arabella. 'Ave you two looked in the mirrah lately?'

Lucy helped Arabella to a larger sofa in the pub so she could rest, and she spent the next half-hour swooning as soon as someone entered to see how things were, and another swearing vengeance on Harold, who was busy guzzling recuperative drinks at the bar.

'Get Harold in here,' she said at last. 'The charlatan!'

He stumbled in. 'Call a black cab, Harold. You are taking me home. From the look of that girl you must have done very well on your walks abroad. Did she play your skin flute? You cad!'

He came close and she draped herself about him. They walked away to a patter of applause.

'You have to tell me everything and answer all my questions before you can be rehabilitated, Harold,' she said.

'I will, my love. It was such fun. She's a sweet, young thing, but will never be as fine an actress as you. I liked the diversion by way of the coins.' Arabella giggled with gratitude.

Lucy and I waited until their cab arrived, and were embarrassed and fascinated to be privy to their little tête-à-tête.

'I couldn't bear to see that artificial little filly clawing at you with her diabolical hands,' Arabella said.

'She's really charming, Arabella. Her fantasy is that she is Eliza Dolittle and I am her Professor Higgins.'

We were astounded to hear Arabella say, 'If that is all it is, I don't see why I should object. You are only civilising her, or is she always wet and ready?' He ignored her last remark with an unconvincing grin.

'Thank you, old girl. I'll seek her out as soon as you're safely tucked-up in bed. You don't mind being alone tonight, do you?'

'I won't, Harold, I'll escape my loneliness and I know you can't run any more. Your heart is against you.'

They laughed like two children at play.

In all the excitement, I had no chance to question Lucy any further about her researches – and I had still said nothing about my ancestry.

CHAPTER THIRTEEN

For several days no one saw either Arabella or her worse half. It seemed that the host and the parasite vine had both vanished.

Finbar, on the other hand, had reappeared, accompanied somewhat to our surprise by his old flame, Benedicta. Acquainted with the latest goings-on, he sat stroking his chin. 'I haven't seen Arabella since I got back, but I did see Harold sitting on the grass on the Heath, blowing up a life-sized doll. Then some kids citizen-arrested him for the molestation of a plastic woman. From my experience of children who frequent parks, I was sure they knew how to handle him.'

I believed every word until Finbar said he was only joking, and that Arabella and Harold must have gone to ground together. After a week, Lucy, Judy and I decided that some investigation as to Arabella's whereabouts was necessary.

'While you're at work on your ancestors, I'll slip away and try to find Arabella,' I informed Lucy. She was going to the British Library to find out more about the Thistlewoods.

'I have an address for her in the East End somewhere. I'll give it to you now,' Lucy replied.

The search for Arabella was not to be just yet. The very next day she phoned at seven a.m., which is when I dream! I was at that very moment giving a real tongue-lashing to Darwin, and threatening him with the treadmill. Lucy had been telling me that this was how her ancestor punished his slaves. I still had not brought myself to tell her I was well acquainted with the cruel history of my own island.

'Hello!' My voice was a mixture of sleep and irritability.

'Alfred! You sound drunk.'

'Arabella! Where have you been?'

At the sound of her name, Sheba jumped on the bed and knocked the phone out of my hand, barking and whining in turns, as she listened to her friend. With some irritation I retrieved the phone.

'See,' laughed Arabella, 'Sheba loves me.'

I said something. I can't now recall.

'Yes, yes, my darling. I have been remiss,' Arabella chortled. 'I know, but needs must. Harold is not well and I cannot leave him. I have forbidden him from seeing his playmate and now he is ill.'

Sheba was panting, as if anxious to ask after Arabella's own health. I tickled her under the chin and she skittered like a lamb over the bed and got into her basket.

'I'm going away, Alfred. I don't know when, and where is not to be disclosed.'

'Then why have you called me?'

'I must either die of shame or disappear. And there's a little problem with the tax man to add to our fun. Luckily Shaddy, an old friend of ours, is over from South Africa, where he went as a doctor, and then fell into diamonds. He deals in them. When I told him what Harold had done, he was so outraged, he offered me a trip.'

'What will become of Honey?'

'I can't leave her with the culprit, that's certain. I might take her. Depends on where I go. But can you imagine her languishing in quarantine kennels after my return? I really can't leave her behind. I'll have to wait and see.'

'Who are these men?'

'Shadrach Moore is one of Harold's buddies – school, army, club and all the rest. When they fantasise they both dress up as matrons. That's how close they are.'

'Are you coming over this way soon? Perhaps we could talk things over.'

'I'll keep you posted.'

I was determined to see her anyway; it was so unlike her not to show up, especially after what she would describe as one of Harold's 'rumpuses' – which always sounded to me like an incident involving an encounter with a strange animal.

I pulled out the address Lucy had given me. '16 Moriarty Close', to which Jamsey had added, 'Down East somewhere, close by some wharf-houses where they hold rave-dances and music fings and where Sherlock Holmes used to go.'

I found the district all right after a dozen or so versions of 'Never 'eard of it, mate', or 'Sherlock 'Olmes topped him years ago'. I was about to think that Arabella had concocted the address, when a decrepit old man directed me to an abandoned railway siding where a ramshackle house stood surrounded by rubbish, piles of tin-cans and an apology for a garden. I pushed the door open. It squeaked, but within Arabella did not move. She was intently polishing her toenails, feet raised on one stool, her pedicure accessories on another.

'Please, ma'am, is Miz Arabella resident here?'

'Yes,' she replied without turning round, 'this is the domicile of Lady Arabella of the Dumpage. Who is it that seeks an audience?'

'Hello, it took some effort to find you.'

'Oh, it's you, Alfred. You're welcome but I cannot remember inviting you round. Did Harold? Go through – he's in there.'

I obeyed. Harold lay, eyes closed, on a fair-sized bed.

'Are you OK, Harold? You look quite flushed. You need a doctor.'

'I have one on call, old boy. I was just rehearsing for death. I drank too much last night. That's all. We were out on the tiles. Shadrach Moore and my brother, Tobias

Quinn – mother's second marriage and all that – Arabella and I.'

'I think you need a doc.'

'Shaddy *is* one. I'm not sure if he's coming round. He'd be delighted if I croaked. He'd be off with Arabella.'

Nothing had changed for them since they were eighteen. In their heads they were still bright young things.

Arabella walked into Harold's room. 'I've had breakfast. Honey ate the last of the caviar on toast. Make the most of what you find,' she said. She pinned me to her gaze like a scrap of gristle on a toothpick as she left the room. They were not living in poverty, they were daring society, cocking a snook at convention. Harold's cough rattled like a barrel organ.

'Oh, Harold, you sound frightfully ill. Steady on.'

'Not really, old boy. It's the vodka. It gets to me! Brings on my problem – ulcers, you see.'

'How is Arabella coping?'

'Oh, well! Too well. She won't let me out of her sight. With you here it would be useful to try and make off!'

He got up, drank his lukewarm coffee and ate some cold toast. He disappeared while I looked at the charcoal and pastel drawings pinned up around the room. Ten minutes later he returned looking better. He had washed and shaved.

'Are the paintings yours, Harold?' I said.

'Most certainly. I dabbled in my salad days. I drew pictures and all the girls became my friends for my charcoal and pastel efforts.'

Arabella, whom I had really come to see, was, I thought, still outside in what was their living room. Her dressing-up clothes hung from a line stretched across the room. Draughts blowing gently through crevices under the window made some of her skirts flutter as if reminding you of their dancing days. Arabella had gone, Honey, too. A note on the table said: 'Must go and have a talk with Shaddy and Toby. See you later, Harold. Remember how ill you are. Be heroic!

Allow Alfred to baby-sit you.' As a signature she had drawn a smiling mouth of reassurance – or perhaps of mockery.

Harold and I went outside. There was the sound of voices and people working in the nearby warehouses.

'What is that place?'

'A kennel factory,' Harold explained. 'Bespoke and expensive doggie hardware for shipment to dog-haters all over the world. People who treat dogs the way Arabella does Honey cannot possibly love them. She believes dogs are children!'

I thought of the WARNING I had been sent by Fynn's and said no more.

'Let's take a walk, old man, down to the *Pig and Whistle*, my favourite pub. We will have a ploughman's lunch there. You'll pay, I trust. Short of the old readies.'

'I hear Arabella is going on a trip.'

'Fantasy, old boy. Neither Shaddy nor Toby will cough up. They moan about us living here rent-free as it is. They're two crooks. They wouldn't know the truth if it bit them in the arse. They wouldn't care if the hawks got us out of here by the scruff.'

'You'll be rehoused.'

'Don't joke, Alfred! We aren't priority. We can't show cause except workless middle age. We are unhelpable. No use pirouetting through pretence like darling Arabella.'

'What will you do?'

'If you mean when the tax muggers come? I'll throw my hands in the air while they search me for loot and after they've gone, I'll swim out until I reach the ocean.'

'You're in a morbid mood today, Harold.'

'Life is morbid but people call that by different aliases.'

We left the house and went to the pub.

We were only halfway through our lunch when Arabella entered with two men. One was a tall, elderly handsome man, with a face that had seen very good times, whose hair was only slightly receding. He had an aura of ruthless strength, with one of those 'See here!' and 'Get me this!' and 'Don't be such an upstart!' voices. From the way the short, stout man waddled behind Mr Authority, I knew that he was Tobias, brother of Harold.

Arabella sat between them and totally ignored us, but Honey didn't. She fought her way out of Arabella's arms and into Harold's.

'You're a good girl, Honey, aren't you?' He kissed her firmly on the nose. Arabella and her friends made their way to the garden to enjoy the sunshine and cold beer. Her interest in her husband seemed more water than milk. I indicated that I would have to be going.

'Come along, old fellow! Honey and I will see you to the bus stop.' What a peculiar couple they were! I couldn't help wondering whether Lucy and I were thought peculiar as well. My thoughts surrounded me like exclamation marks all the way home.

When at last I reached my house, Arabella called to say she was sorry we had not spoken, but she was trying to pin down Shadrach as to her cruise.

'How did you get on?' I asked.

'A hiatus was the order of the day. Neither of the two misers would cough up. They would for a day in Brighton, but that's not for me.'

'Just be patient. Honey would pine for you, so perhaps it's all for the best.'

'The fourth tea-dance will be on the doorstep soon,' she observed.

'Will you attend? Won't it be the last for this year?'

'You must wait and see.'

'You'll have to face the gossip, Arabella. They would love to hold you down. Don't let them.'

'Oh, I won't! They won't! I'm sure of it.'

When I next went to the park, Judy had some sad news for us. Uncle Nat had died. He had been getting more frail by the day and had been coming to the park less frequently. He was always saying to us that the Lord was now calling him home, and he'd soon be going. He'd see his young wife again and his beloved kin from Sierra Leone. It would be a joyful occasion so we shouldn't mourn. Even so, we were shocked and grieved. Judy, who visited him frequently, took him food and sat with him, said he'd passed so peacefully.

We said our farewells to Uncle Nat a couple of days later. It was a splendid affair, and in truth we were surprised because Uncle Nat had looked so poor. His hearse was drawn by plumed horses, his coffin hidden in flowers and the pallbearers wore black top hats with hanging crepe ribbons. The procession went slowly round the streets surrounding the park, before leaving for the cemetery. Hundreds of people gathered to say their goodbyes. Uncle Nat had been well loved.

The very next day a different invitation, one to Judy's birthday party, arrived via Finbar. It was going to be special – huge, according to Finbar, with the world and his wife and every Tom, Dick and Harry, from near and far, attending.

'Why all the fuss?'

'She is going to be fifty. Blessed, semi-aged fifty.'

'She doesn't look a day over forty-two or three,' I said. 'Lucy would be green with envy. She looks fifty and she isn't. All that grey hair! She should do something about it.'

'Let's go to the Pizza Place. Man to man for a change,' Finbar invited.

I suddenly felt hungry and we headed round the corner to the restaurant. It was pleasant and homely with little corners of palms and flowers. The salad bar looked formidable: crisp lettuce, newly prepared tomatoes, sliced cucumbers and other treats. I helped myself to a heaped bowl, and managed half of my pizza. Finbar ate a whole giant pizza, burped loudly and said, 'There's a hungry man for you! Judy wants to hold her party in the pub. We'll have a band with fiddlers, a sound system and songs and things. Benedicta will be coming.'

'Benedicta, the love of your life?'

'Over the hill and ravaged by time,' he chuckled. 'Time has stolen everything from her. She had two lovely melons for breasts and large firm pumpkins for backsides. Oh! Oh! how pretty they were. When I think of women past and gone I always recall their pretty parts.'

We paid our bill and went back to Lucy's. She was out with our dogs.

I lay on the settee and nodded off, as old men do. I woke to find Lucy standing over me.

'Finbar left as soon as I came back. He said you snore like a desert camel.'

'I've never heard a camel snore!' She smiled. For the first time I noticed that her teeth were thin and long, like miniature off-white picket fences... I loved them! I loved her! I wanted to confess this to someone, anyone, except her, for fear of the effect it would have on both of us.

'Judy and I went on the Heath with the dogs, and afterwards hitched them to a post in the shade and bought ourselves cool and refreshing cocktails.'

I was just about to confess my love but she ran on. 'Who should be hidden in corner seats? Those two "twinky" sisters, Martha and Dorinda Belle – they danced together at tea-dance. Judy and I wouldn't have noticed them if they had kept their mouths shut. They were discussing – guess who? – Arabella. They said she was a liberty-taker, and Harold a henpecked clown. Judy rebuked them for condemning friends in the "ears of God". They got up and abruptly stamped off as guilty as thrown stones.'

'It's the way women are, Lucy. They chew over old bones. Come here.'

She opened her arms wide as if to enclose me and then slowly put her palms together and simpered, 'Not here!

There,' she said pointing to her bedroom. 'The children might come in! Whatever will we tell them?' We giggled like two-year-olds.

Lucy never failed to amuse me. I began to recognise that she was beginning to take the place once occupied by Florence – my friend, lover, critic and mother. A pang of guilt went through me, but I knew that my life had moved on. Lucy and I would have no children but we had our dogs – our neutered memories and easy-flowing intimacies. We spent much time in the kind of loving that had become a routine delight, and it was the intensity of that delight that was driving me to propose to her. I vowed to do it next time we were in bed.

It rained on Thursday. Rainy Thursdays are no good for proposals. It continued to rain as if Fate was giving me respite. I was beginning to worry about Sheba's exercise routine. The park was not what it used to be. The community had become unstable. People talked of parks where the lavatories were better. Finbar, Jamsey, Judy and I were the only faithful remnants of the original park people. Lucy, Arabella and Harold pleased themselves: frequent visitors at some times, and absentees at others.

I thought of the park as it used to be: Declan and Maisie fighting or loving, Old Thomack grumbling, Uncle Nat preaching. Rootsman running, Maryanne in spasms on the grass and crepuscular bats and beetles flashing past at twilight.

The daily visitors had been important too. Uncle Nat's nameless friend with his polystyrene bed hanging from his back, and the tall handsome Indian man, Doc, who entertained us with his immigrant stories. Doc was the man who, when told he had no proof of torture by his political enemies, disrobed in the waiting room. His wounds had not yet healed. His back was burnt and raw. His official inquisitors fled. We had seen little of Doc, recently.

Some things had not changed. We still drank tea, marinated in condensed or evaporated milk, and still enjoyed ourselves. I believed, though, that the curtains were coming down on this stage in my life, on a place where the grass was greener than in my garden.

Lucy spent each morning writing up her findings about her ancestor of 'Worthy Park', Jamaica.

'When I am finished at the Public Records and the British Library, I'll show you my notes and then perhaps we can visit Jamaica. I once did, with Jacobus, but he was such a bigot. He wanted to live there and trade on his white skin.'

'As you wish, my dear. I'm in no hurry.'

'I'll be a while, Alfred. Read something of what I've already found out, while I go on with my work.'

I prowled about looking for her notes. Was I a secret bigot by trading on my skin? My silence about my Africa had been common sense in the past. It ensured me access to jobs which even a suspicion of being part African might have denied me. It had become a habit, my Englishness a comfortable coat, though from time to time I had wondered whether it was really mine, and whether I was losing some part of myself. Later, when the colour of men's and women's skins became much less of a bar to opportunity, I should no doubt have made my identity open. But it was also a time when pride in blackness was the order of the day, and what place was there in that world for someone like me? I barely fitted the much criticised category of 'Afro-Saxon'. I was certainly the latter, but of my Africanness there was no more visible than a slight Mediterranean tinge. It was only more recently in the park that the masks of convenience and habit had grown to feel uncomfortable. The park embraced all shades, all cultures. Why had I never revealed myself? My discomfort had been most acute when I'd been with Maryanne and Rootsman. She had touched something deep in me, reminded me that one of my ancestors had been like her – vulnerable and abused as Maryanne had been. It had inwardly galled me too when Rootsman, not unkindly, dismissed my offers of help for her as coming from a whiteman.

As I looked for Lucy's notes, I knew I would have to find the moment to say something. What I found came from the earliest period of her research. Her handwriting, when I truly noticed it, was round and clear – easy to read – not what I had expected. Later pieces of her writing had the unmistakeable stamp of urgency and agitation. I read:

My ancestor, Thomas Thistlewood, born in 1741. He arrived aged 29 years in Jamaica from Lincolnshire. He worked as an cattle-pen keeper and then an overseer at a plantation close to Savanna La Mar. He was sexually voracious, different from other planters only in one important respect – he kept a lifelong diary about his life and aggressive sexual predations on his women . From a page of his diary I have taken a few examples recorded in English and Latin. He had pretensions to being a scholarly man and once invited the novelist and builder of follies, William Beckford, to a dinner at which he served mutton broth, roast mutton and broccoli, carrots, asparagus, stewed mud-fish, roast goose and paw-paw, apple sauce, stewed giblets, some fine lettuce and much more while his slaves roamed around the estate trying to find food of any kind. It is clear that the African slaves were the foundation of all plantation riches but treated like disposable beasts of burden. A sample from his diary:

"I enjoy'd Marina, my wife first (super lect cum Marina) then Flora, a congo-girl, was next (super terram)".

My ancestor was unspeakably brutal in the choice of punishments. He chose the vilest ways to humiliate men, women and children. I cannot be sure whether he was corrupted by slavery or the culture in which it flourished, or because slavery drew more than usually corruptible people to it.

I am ashamed of my lineage and would have been more so, had

not one of my ancestor's descendants, Arthur Thistlewood, one of the
countless children he inflicted upon the slave women, fought and died
in the cause of freedom for the poor. I undertook this study to know
my past, though whether my descent is from Thomas, as my father
boasted, or from Arthur, as I would like to believe, I may never know.

I was quite surprised by the emotions running through Lucy's comments. Words like swine, blackguard, culprit were frequent. I asked myself whether ancestral voices resided in people who show hatred and aversion to other races. If Lucy's ancestor was Thomas Thistlewood, she had certainly not inherited his racial attitudes. But as I read more of these annals of brutality, feelings of despondency and odours of times long gone floated out of some deep crapulent pool inside me. It was a past which I did not care to look back to. I was well aware that those sections of the Grayson family which had assiduously whitened themselves regarded the darker Graysons with embarrassed contempt. When I thought about that and the comfortable, self-regarding prejudices of the Barbadian middle classes from which I came, a trapdoor opened under me. It led straight to Thomas Thistlewood raping Flora, the Congo-girl, on the ground. Her face, when I imagined it, was Maryanne's.

Lucy evidently felt that by genealogy she inherited the guilt of her distant ancestor's crimes. This was nonsense, I thought, and I would tell her so. My complicity in the privileges of whiteness was much more real.

When Lucy returned and I told her she should not get involved in the Thistlewood past if it upset her so much, that she had no reason for feeling guilty, she flew into a violent rage, as if I had lashed her and rubbed brine into the cuts. I discovered I had not really understood what had driven her.

'Look, I was brought up to be proud of the Thistlewoods. It was all I really had of distinction. I used to introduce myself as Lucy McAlpine née Thistlewood. Discovering the truth about them has been part of facing up to the truth about my family life. For years I blanked out that my father was evil to me. He wanted a son. He got me. All he ever told my mother was how useless she was, and me how duffy and ugly I was. My mother left us. She could not take me. Men were the breadwinners then; children stayed with them. I lost touch with my mother completely. I never even knew whether she was alive or dead. So, there I was, living with someone who took not the slightest interest in me. His sister and I went shopping once every few months. He farmed me out after the war. They were good people but I did not know affection, though I pretended otherwise. Marriage was an escape for me.' Here her voice passed into a piercing minor key.

'When I look back on my father he was cold and unloving. He hated anyone not of England and showed them his cold contempt. I would never have heard of my ancestor, Thomas Thistlewood, had my father not boasted of his eminence and wealth. I knew he had owned plantations in Jamaica, but had not understood how cruelly gotten that wealth had been. I realised that my father, in his own smaller way, had the same capacity for cruelty as our illustrious ancestor. My husband was little better. And I had tried to pretend to myself that this wasn't so. It is painful, but I have to face the truth. The Thistlewoods thought they had the right because they were white and because they were men. I see now that the way I was treated by my father and my husband connects in some way with how Thomas Thistlewood felt he could treat his slaves.'

'But does it really matter now, Lucy? Who cares what colour anyone is?'

'Nonsense! Cloud Cuckoo-Land. White is White!' she shouted. 'And that still decides who wins most of life's prizes.'

I suddenly felt locked into a white room with jet black windows too small for me to escape. I fought for breath and said, 'White isn't always what it seems. I've never told you that I originally came here from Barbados. I came from the light-skinned side of a family with brown and black cousins. We came in three shades. I don't flay myself. When the ozone layer flips, melanin will reign. Everyone will be out shopping for it.'

Lucy was looking at me so steadily that I felt this flippancy was not in order.

'I always knew my family had black forebears. My great, great grandmother was a slave, who bore four children for her owner. After emancipation, he sold his plantation, turned them all out and with the money started a bank that exists to this day. The moral of this story is that all white is not white.'

'But why have you been so reluctant to tell me this, Alfred? Why should you have kept this to yourself?'

'It's a complex story, I suppose. I came to England when landlords advertised 'No Coloureds' and when well-qualified West Indians could only get jobs on the buses. As someone who passed for white, it was much simpler to be white. As time went by I became more English, which wasn't hard. Barbados was always the most English of the islands – it was known as Bimshire – and my family prided itself on how anglicised it was.'

'You are a dark one,' Lucy said.

I laughed.

Lucy made some coffee which we drank in reflective silence.

'Give the dogs their biscuits, please, Alfred. Their looks could turn me to stone any minute now,' she said at last.

CHAPTER FOURTEEN

Judy's party was on everybody's list of 'musts', but the surging waters of the fourth tea-dance, with all its rapids and hidden boulders, had first to be negotiated. We decided not to entrust our frail craft to the tea-dance torrents. On my part, I was undecided as to whether we should still be living in two separate spaces, whether we should still be pretending to our friends that our life together did not exist.

On the tea-dance day, warm as the breath of a sleeping dog, Lucy and I decided to take a boat trip from Westminster pier. It was a fair ride to get there but worth the effort. The boat was full but not crowded and, comfortably seated, we listened as a true East Ender relayed the history of his home base. Disembarking at Greenwich, we headed for the park. We'd been told that there would be summer celebrations there. We ate silly fare like candyfloss, toffee apples and lollipops like a pair of kids. Behind us the river flowed like reams of beaded beige silk, chortling and coruscating in the sunlight. The clouds, active at the edges and flirting with the wind, created new shapes every time I looked up. It was a trip I wished would last for hours.

We wandered along the High Street, up side streets, past shops of all kinds. At last we found the park and were just in time to see a puppet show in progress. The child in many adults was shouting, 'Let down your hair!' when the Rapunzel puppet began to let down unending coils of blonde braids to a huge, soft, doll lover.

'You'll never get your leg over!' someone called. 'It's too short!' It was amusing but not to my taste. We wandered from show to show until from behind a screen of holly we heard unmistakably familiar accents. What had drawn us was the song being played. It was the 'Tennessee Waltz', a tune that Arabella adored and frequently played on her tape recorder as we sat and drank our tea.

'Can it be them?' Lucy asked.

'They never miss a chance to show off, but I'm surprised they're not at the tea-dance.'

The music stopped to polite – very polite – applause and we peeped in and there they were: the dancing pair. Arabella was explaining to the onlookers that their next dance would have to be shortened because it was so warm.

We made our escape, but not fast enough.

'Heavens!' Lucy blurted out. 'They're tracking us.' Honey seemed to have scented us, and was sniffing in our direction. Arabella, whirling in her dress of apricot frills, and Harold in his white suit watched helplessly as Honey ran off at full speed.

'Come here, Honey!' Harold yelled as he continued to step it out with Arabella. Honey ran through the audience. Suddenly a hand popped out of the crowd, snatched up Honey and scolded, 'Where ya going! Can't you see your mum and dad are busy?' It was Felicia.

Honey, wilful brat, growled in pique.

We eyed them through the trees, but Honey still had our scent. She wriggled free again, and came sniffing and piddling on my shoes as she so often did. Harold followed.

'However did you two hear of this? Shaddy arranged it. It came as a total surprise to us. It's nice of you to show up. Shaddy and Toby are having a few days in France. Did they telephone?'

'How could they? They aren't our friends.'

'Oh, there's Felicia,' exclaimed Lucy.

'Y-a-ss,' said Harold breathlessly. 'She came to help us and baby-sit Honey. Y-a-ss. I think it's spot on that Toby fancies her.'

119

'Are you brothers involved in team games with young ladies? Well, no matter, old chap! Why aren't you two dancing your toes off at the tea-dance?

'Gave them the slip, old boy! Told them to go to hell. The day is too warm to be cooped up with bloody fossils, present company excluded.'

Arabella had now escaped from her admirers and came to us.

'We escaped – Shaddy helped us. Those vipers will go home with their venom sacs half-used.'

'I thought Shaddy wouldn't cough anything up,' said Lucy.

'He did eventually, and here we are! How did you two get here?'

'By boat and we're just off to make the return trip.'

'We rented a car. A lift is in order,' said Harold.

'Our dogs are waiting. We go by boat.'

Lucy was pensive all the way back. At last she spoke. 'There was a letter came this morning. I know it's from Jacobus, my ex. I haven't opened it yet. I didn't want it to spoil our day. But I'll have to look at it.'

When we reached Lucy's, our dogs, heads together, looked out of the window that faced the path. In a frenzy of delight they barked and danced their rapture at our appearance. We were very tired after the day's outing and I thought it best to leave Lucy alone to read her letter. I went home to think about the day.

Early the next morning the doorbell rang. There were voices outside, those of the dancing duo. I recalled that, thanks to Toby or Shaddy or both, they had a car at their disposal.

'A moment!' I called out. But they did not hear. They were having a gigantic row.

'I know, I know!' Harold shouted angrily. 'I tell you the truth, my life's a burden.'

'If you want to die, Harold, don't fuss about it, just do it!'

'Don't be so cruel, Arabella!'

'Darling, I'm not being cruel. I don't want you to have pain. Just tell Judy we'll dance for her... You're being unreasonable. You're not being flogged, for heaven's sake.'

I opened the door.

'Hello, you two!'

'We're not coming in,' Arabella blurted. 'We went round to Judy's but she's out. Tell her to call me, please, Alfred. It's urgent.'

They left hurriedly in their hired car.

It began to rain slowly at first and then it poured. Some summer! I telephoned Judy several times and concluded that she had gone out. Around midday I called again. She was still out. I called Lucy. She, too, did not reply. Fear froze my entrails. What if she had gone off with her ex?

Time seemed endless. The hours crawled by. I steeled myself, picked up the phone, whistled into it for luck, dialled her number, quickly dropped the phone and finally decided to go to her house at the crack of dawn the next day.

My feelings were fraught with the fear of rejection and betrayal. Lucy did not speak as she let me in. There were remnants of tears in her eyes.

'What's up?'

She smiled weakly. 'I'm sorry for myself; take no notice.'

I sat beside her. Sad-faced, her emotions tight inside her, she pressed her face into my chest and sobbed dryly, a repressed sob, as if she was trying hard not to cough up the horrors she had been remembering.

'He wants to see me. For what I do not know. He's staying at a hotel not far from here – *The Moonglow*. He's evidently not short of money. I just don't know whether to go. It will be hard to see him, but I think I ought to – and I'm curious to see what time and life have done to him.'

'Has he a wife?'

'No, she died some time ago – of pneumonia. She caught it after he'd pushed her into a duck pond during one of his rages.'

'Perhaps he has come to reclaim you! Did he really do that?' Every time she spoke of him I hated him more. No doubt he was richer than ever.

She looked at me, pulled me close and kissed me tenderly. 'I want to spend all my days and nights with you,' she said. 'I don't know whether I'll see Jacobus again, but I'll tell you if decide to go.'

For a moment I was lost in memory and heard the soft music I associated with my dear wife's face when I first kissed her under the moon on Margate sands. Then I looked into Lucy's eyes and at that instant I saw in her life pain after pain after pain. Unloved by her father, treated cruelly by her husband and abandoned by her mother. She sat there for a moment as solitary and as mournful as a manatee.

'Would you like to see my party dress?' she remarked, perking up. 'I always wanted a birthday party but never had one until my brief wedding breakfast, and that was like dining with Scrooge before his reformation.'

'Surprise me, Lucy, when you wear your new dress to the party. I'm certain you'll look dazzling in it. Have you anything to post? I'm off to the post office.' Relief had suddenly stirred me. Gave me a sneaky hard-on. They had become more and more frequent at each meeting with Lucy. But at that moment I thought that Lucy needed time to herself.

'Just a book of stamps, if you don't mind.'

I walked down the street, still trying to piece together where our relationship stood. The restaurants, which had proliferated, made me feel hungry, but I pressed on, anonymous as usual, except when in the park. When I returned with her stamps she had gone out. It was nearly ten. Just time to catch Jamsey making tea in the park. They were all there and, from the laughter, I knew that Arabella had arrived and was in fine form.

As the tea brewed Arabella asked, 'Are you going to be there tomorrow?'

'Lucy will be the voice of the proceedings, like those men who call themselves Master of Ceremonies.'

'Finbar will call Judy's toast and then we'll be left to enjoy ourselves, except when Harold and I dance 'The Green Grass Tango' in memory of Barker and Uncle Nat.'

'Wouldn't that be out of place?'

'Don't be so suburban, Alfred. We are dog lovers, primitive in our choices, bucolic in our need of company. Dogs, deer, horses are for us. Whatever civilisation bids us become, we are itinerants at heart. We prefer to travel with our animals than to arrive with humans.'

'Hear hear!' Finbar's new sidekick Sean chirped. 'Even if I don't know what you mean, Arabella, I like dogs better than people – present company included.' He laughed unendingly at his jokes. He had suddenly appeared and attached himself like a bun-shaped limpet to Finbar.

The company joined in. They laughed at everything, as if everything contained essences of smut. To me the park contained elements of heaven and of hell, which people accepted either with a frown, or a laugh, a tear, a scream or with silence.

'Judy,' I said, 'deserves respect from us all and the night of her fiftieth birthday would be a good time to show how much we respect her.'

'That's a good point, Alfred,' Arabella said. 'We all tend to be frivolous and let our hair down, especially in the park. We must not gobble up the goodies she has prepared. We must eat them with due appreciation.'

We broke into bits of conversation. Arabella would not describe her proposed outfit, though normally she would have been only too keen.

'Allow me to surprise you. Harold will be in his black evening suit and, of course, his red cummerbund. He always looks so divine.'

'Will brother Toby be there?'

'Shaddy might, if he gets back in time. It's years since we danced together. I hope he comes.'

'And Toby?'

'He's off out with Felicia. She's so sweet. I think Toby is helping himself to her sugar – wherever she keeps it.'

'I thought you hated her guts,' prodded Finbar.

'Of course, but not all the time.'

Arabella was so transparent. Though she played games and had her little stratagems, she would not know real deception if it crawled up the seam of her stockings and nipped her bum.

We dispersed to prepare for Judy's big night. Lucy had indicated she would be out, helping Judy. 'There's a lot to be done.' Benedicta would be helping too. 'She's a lovely woman. Just like a Beryl Cook painting with plump arms and legs and body parts that could fit only into circles.' The park was full of circles, triangles and squares – people, ideas and hopes all with their different shapes.

Suddenly a daring thought hopped into my mind. What if I tried to make a circle of our triangle – Lucy, me and Jacobus? What if I went and chatted to him? I might find out his true intentions – and possibly encourage him to leave Lucy alone. She was so torn about whether to see him or not. If he left that would solve her problems.

I got on a bus and hopped off at the Moonglow Hotel where Jacobus was staying. It was about three o'clock and I entered the restaurant to have tea. Lucy had said he took tea each afternoon. I would recognise him from her description – tall, angular, heavy eyebrows, protruding jaws and inquisitive eyes.

I hadn't long to wait. Tall and carrying a floating paunch that heaved above the belt of his khaki trousers, he walked cautiously with the help of a cane. He wore eyeshades. My throat constricted and my stomach lurched. Lucy walked beside him. Without stopping even to draw up her chair and help her to her seat, Jacobus sat down leaving her to fend for herself. She did not seem to mind and poured the tea after it was brought. She placed the sandwiches under his hand. She was extremely solicitous. Why had she kept this visit from me? I was growing angrier by the minute. I had to find out why she said one thing to me and was acting otherwise. I rose from my chair and went over to them.

'Hello Lucy!'

She looked startled but managed a smile. 'Hello, Alfred. Fancy seeing you here. This is Jacobus. He can't see you. He's blind. This is Alfred Grayson, Jacobus, a really good friend.'

His hand shook so much when he reached for sugar it was if he was playing a tune with the spoon on the bowl.

'Alfred and I plan to marry.' She winked at me.

'I can tell from your voice that you're dependable. A man of your word and a lover of animals. Good luck to you. Lucy, what I wanted from you must now remain untold. I must find other solutions.' He rose at once. Fumbled his way about the chairs until he reached the entrance and then, declining all help, called out, 'Goodbye, Lucy. I'm off tomorrow,' and up the stairs he went.

'Why did you come, Alfred? I didn't know he'd lost his sight, poor man!'

The clock struck five as we went home.

'Jacobus did not take tea,' I observed.

'He was agitated. Too much to drink,' she replied.

From time to time, she cracked open her thoughts and exclaimed, in a voice dripping with sorrow, 'I never knew! What could I have done? I thought he was going to ask me to come back to him. It would have been terrible to refuse.'

'No one knows why these things happen, but they do. Be his friend! That's all we can both be!'

'Hold me, Alfred! Hold me so that I can let go of these awful thoughts I have about him.'

'Poor Lucy. Don't shiver so!' I kissed her there and then in the street she was so tearful. 'Let's think of nobler and more enjoyable times to come. We're too old for public capering and displays.'

'You're not going to leave me hanging on like a leaf with a broken stalk? You're what I want, not tea. I feel so restless. So bottled up, and yet exposed.'

'We'll soon be home.'

Florence used to feel bottled up too. But when she was angry about anything there was no intimacy of any sort between us. Not even a cup of tea in bed. For us, tea was always the start of intimacy and on occasions I was sure I heard it rushing about inside me as we made love – like the sound of a hot water bottle.

There was no tea when we arrived home. Just bed and the blessed relief of tensions and a rediscovery of each other. Satiated, we sat silent and smiling hand in hand and naked, our legs hanging over the side of the bed. Wordless feelings of love rose inside me – and plunges of anxiety. Was she insatiable? What if I died?

Dressed at last, I let the dogs out of their gated patch of garden and fed them. Sheba was in a foul mood, nipping Mutt's tail and haggling over biscuits and scraps of meat. Sheba liked to spend time alone and too much dog-company always irritated her.

'Very well, old girl. I'll take you home,' I promised.

'Where shall we meet?' Lucy asked. 'I'm helping Judy set out the food. There's mountains of it. '

'I hope she can afford it.'

'Didn't she tell you? Uncle Nat left her a few thousand pounds for her kindness, and she wants to share it with all who knew him. He left thousands of pounds to a church that saved his life. I'll be home around four. I'll have a rest and then get set for eight.'

'You're a fine woman, Lucy, deserving of all that's wonderful in life.'

I dressed with great care, patted and smoothed what was left of my hair, straightened my tie, ducked and dived in front of the mirror, wished I had a valet to give my jacket a final brush and strode out into the night. I felt complete. When I reached the venue, the club attached to the local pub, smartly dressed men and women were already gathered. Alana, relaxed and well-groomed, looked like a crisp, new, fashion plate. Long gone was the doggie patter, the trade babble. Like me, no part of her body was lying fallow. She, too, was in love, I was sure of it.

Judy was surrounded by her guests and that gave me time to view her cards and presents. She looked radiant in navy blue. It slimmed her down and made her look no older than forty, which flattered her when remarked upon. There were cards from scores of people I did not know but I recognised Maryanne's, and those from Declan, Maisie and family, Benedicta, Mr Thomack, Jah Garside and many, many others.

There were presents from the dogs, though their owners handed them over. I felt sorry that Lucy and I had not brought our dogs but Finbar put on a record of dogs barking 'Happy Birthday to You' as a small consolation!

He had the charming Benedicta on his arm. Lucy said she showed off, but that was her way – open, free-flowing and assertive.

He winked at me as I wished Judy fifty more years. 'How do you like Benedicta?' he whispered. 'She's a very nice and loving woman. I can vouch for that. And deep as the ocean in body and mind.' I winked back in the suggestive style of men.

On the stroke of eight, Lucy called for order. She welcomed us all, talked of the significance of the great five-O, the halfway house of life. Speeches fell like corn in the barnyard, toasts were called and drunk as often as was necessary, and 'Good Wishes' flowed interminably. Then Lucy asked the folk dancers to make their contribution for our enjoyment. They danced with a precise rhythm, easy to enjoy, and then they sang, 'Molly Malone', Judy's favourite schooldays' tune. I recalled the dramatic tattoos her dress concealed and wondered what the crowd would make of them if she revealed them. The swirling hand-painted neck-wrap hid everything. I was grateful to have seen it – touched it, rubbed myself against it.

It was time for Judy to take the floor for her birthday waltz, for which I was chosen to partner her. I'm no dancer but she carried me along, fine dancer that she was. Then the real dancing began. Recorded music took over and we all danced to The Beatles. At the height of the activity who should appear but Harold, Arabella and Honey.

'Judy,' exclaimed Arabella. 'You look divine in navy. As promised, we have brought you your tango. Call upon us when you're ready. We've danced twice tonight,' she added, 'and Harold's rather breathless. After this we're going home. He mustn't overdo things, but applause is like a delicious food to him. He gorges on it.'

'Give Harold a drink,' said Judy, 'and have one yourself. I'll announce the dance when everyone is stuck into cake or food. Food concentrates the mind.'

A little later Judy went over to Lucy and after a great deal of whispering Lucy put down her glass, clapped her hands and said, 'One item is left for you to enjoy. Sit comfortably and watch the tango, a skilful and beautiful dance in its purest form. Here's tango essence from our champions, Harold and Arabella!'

Arabella and Harold took the floor. She curtsied deeply, he bowed low as she explained, 'This is a celebratory dance, first for us knowing a woman like Judy, for a night like this and to the memory of the dogs that died or were hurt. Come along, Darwin, you killed in public. Now apologise in public. Be a man for once.'

Darwin hobbled out of the shadows where he was trying to be inconspicuous. He was leaning on his walking stick, trying to look like a man who had paid a price for his crimes. He had indeed had his ankle broken by the owners of the

Dalmation he had shot, when they had finally caught up with him. But, according to Finbar, the stick was now merely a ploy for sympathy. Whatever, Darwin came forward and apologised in heartfelt profusion.

'Now you are forgiven. Put the stick away. You skived out of Community Service but we've all heard you now.'

There was a very thin, half-hearted stream of applause. His face bright red, he sobbed as Tina, his loyal girlfriend, comforted him. 'He's going back to college. Give him a chance,' she pleaded. Everyone clapped her loyalty – though it could have been for the couple who had taken the floor.

Harold bowed low once more. Arabella curtsied with elegance and grace. The sequins on her burgundy dress twinkled like fireflies at night. Now we would observe the real richness of the tango, the Green Grass Tango, which Harold had composed especially for the occasion.

The sound of their tape filled the room from the roof to ceiling and exploded into the night. Harold and Arabella danced in perfect harmony, perfect synchrony and perfect grace – the tendril and the host again unified. The onlookers felt the thrill of the tango and clapped and hurrahed. Then Harold began stepping over his own feet. His eyes seemed to have lost focus, his movements unsteady. He staggered and fell, a mass on the floor.

'Oh! What a pain! My chest! Oh!' he murmured. People rushed to him and gently and carefully took him into a quiet room and laid him on a table.

'Get a doctor!' shouted Lucy. 'Such heart and soul dancing is exhausting! He must be exhausted, poor dear!'

'Get Shaddy' Arabella cried. 'He's is in the pub. So are Toby and Felicia.' She circled Harold, wringing her hands, her sobs enriching his harsh, tight breaths.

I found Shaddy, and moments later he was bending over Harold, saying, 'The pulse is faint. Call the ambulance quickly. A private one. Please don't quibble, Toby. He's your only brother.'

After a while Harold was taken out by a side door and handed over to the expensively private paramedics who had been painfully slow in arriving. I thought his heart had given up for good.

'Come along, Shaddy. You being a doctor might help us.' Arabella, overtaken by some fierce resolve, pushed him into the ambulance. 'Bulk or no bulk, you're coming with us.'

Toby, always a follower, also accompanied Harold, leaving Lucy to take Felicia under her wing.

Lucy announced to the assembly, 'Harold has been taken to hospital. He was exhausted and collapsed. I'm sure he will be home tomorrow.'

Everyone clapped, and the tango began again. People danced to the tune as their feet and anxieties allowed. Gone, though, was the grace and style, the harmony of movement and consciousness of space that Arabella and Harold achieved.

Lucy kept everyone's spirits high. Judy wanted to end the party, but Lucy insisted Harold would want the show to go on. 'He'll be home and bouncy by this time next week,' she assured us.

Nevertheless a kind of darkness fell over us all. Hushed voices and sighs of concern touched everything. People began to drift away, after thanking Judy for a lovely time. Finbar, Benedicta, Lucy and I shut ourselves down and went home with Judy. We desperately wanted to know that Harold was all right, but could not find out, as we didn't know to which of several hospitals he might have been taken. We sat silent, wound-up, sad.

'Do you think he overdid it?' Judy said. 'But what a pretty sight they made! Arabella is a lovely dancer – so slim, so agile, such youthful spirit. Only her wrinkles tell the truth.'

We made cups of coffee.

'Youthful spirit?' said Finbar as he slurped his coffee. 'Is that what you call it? She's going to show him the road to the mortuary one of these fine days.'

'I agree with Finbar,' Benedicta said. 'Everybody has to know when to stop. This life is the real one. You can want more than is set for you but you will not get it.'

'This is no mothers' meeting for you to start preaching at,' Finbar said. 'Father O'Hanley always scolded me with these potent words: "There's a Divinity that shapes our ends. Rough hew them how we will". So take note, my girl. God is judge – not mortal man or woman.'

CHAPTER FIFTEEN

The phone rang abruptly, angrily, spitefully, each ring conveying a different emotion. Finbar answered eagerly. It was Arabella. 'Harold has survived his heart attack, thank God. What should I do without him? He's the fire I warm my hands at when they are freezing and myself when I am cold.' As I relayed her words, everybody's face turned red with surprise.

'Hypocrite,' said Finbar.

Lucy said how grateful to God we all were, and that we would go to bed with peace in our hearts.

'Have you got Honey with you?' asked Arabella.

'I think Felicia took her.'

'Felicia! No! Will you get her and maybe Judy will keep her until Monday. I'll come and fetch her then. Please, Alfred,' Arabella begged.

I scurried back to the pub just to make sure. The hall was empty. No sign of Honey, but her basket sat there empty. I gave it a harsh kick. Bloody dog, where could she have gone? I went into the pub to ask if anyone had seen a fussy, dirty-white poodle.

'Yes,' said the landlord. 'Here she is, fast asleep. She done all right. They were all giving her sips of beer and cider. She fell asleep on top of her cider. I had to dry her off. Snappy little thing, ain't she.' His laughter sounded like prolonged gargling.

I fetched her basket. As she slept on, it seemed as if something wicked had been done to her, some wicked prank had been played upon the poor trusting creature.

I hurried her back to Judy's. She held her like a lost child. 'Imagine how she feels with both of them gone.'

'They are not both gone! Why do you expand thinking further than your arms can stretch?' Finbar said with smouldering irritation. 'They're both at the hospital. One sitting up and the other lying down. The dog knows what's up with them,'

In spite of the voices Honey did not move, though when Finbar reassured her that her owner would return, her right ear twitched.

Lucy and I were first to leave. Against my better judgement, I kissed Honey goodbye.

'Come along, Lucy,' I said. 'We'd better find what our dogs are up to.'

She grabbed my hand in anticipation of what was to come. As we walked I heard her heart beating, felt her body ready and rejoicing. I hugged her, held her closer than I had ever done before. She sighed.

'You love me, Alfred, don't you?'

I didn't reply since I never talk love. It is something you live day after mundane, boring, slogging day, something that lasts for some unfortunate wretches an infinity of years. I could hear my father now.

'We've been married for fifty years, sixty years,' he'd say proudly. He failed to add, 'I've been bored a million times, wanted to be tempted ten thousand times, found the sex dull, boring, limp, unsatisfying.'

'Love,' I said, 'is something you live and act each day.' At the moment I loved my dead wife because she couldn't come back, loved Lucy because she filled the gap left by Florence – and loved her for herself. Sometimes I felt I was drawn to love every sad, unhappy woman I met, embrace them all, offer all of them my heart, take them all to bed – and kiss them goodbye on both cheeks. Was there something I should be seeing here? But such thoughts fled as we reached Lucy's doorstep.

I was so full of feelings we had hardly gone inside the house than we began to ransack each other, like burglars in a hurry, hurling off our clothes like a flurry of feathers, recklessly, urgently. There we were, engulfed in desire, with waves so high they would drown us, had we not the skill to ride them and surmount them. At last, as a reward for my endeavour to please, there came that once-in-a-lifetime moment of ecstasy's essence, distilled and pouring out of me like an emission from heaven. My mind dissolved. My tongue faltered. I was in some other place.

'Florrie,' I murmured. 'I do love you. You are God's dearest gift to me.'

Lucy stiffened above me. I suddenly felt as cold as death.

'What did you call me? I heard you distinctly. You spoke to Florence. You said you loved her. You cad, hypocrite and cheat. How could you be so awful?' She burst into a storm of tears.

She sprung off the bed and in next to no time was in the shower.

'Get the hell out of here! For all your airs and graces you are the biggest skunk of all. You don't love me at all.'

'Will you listen to me! Florence is dead – has been for many years. In my mind, just at that moment you became her. But you are the one who's important to me now. But what do you mean by love? It's an overused, blindfolding word. It hooks on to your insides and makes an unreasonable and implacable fool out of people, as you are being now.'

'Get out – you bastard – you lecher. You swine. Get the hell out.'

I took my dog home with me. Just then I felt that Lucy had gone out of my life. Whether there was any coming back we would have to see.

Arabella, who had been calling Lucy, knew something was up. She tried to dig the facts out of me but I did not give way. 'Ask her,' I said.

'Has there been a lovers' quarrel?' she probed.

'Don't pry, Arabella! It's best if you don't get involved.'

Everyone except Finbar was concerned about us. He thought fate had saved me from something which I would rather not mention. 'She's a sex-starved spinster,' Finbar said. 'Spinster in mind but gutter in body.'

'Don't!' I said. 'Remember you were a gentleman once.'

'Yes, forty years ago. This is another time. Have you seen Harold?'

I had never expected to see Harold alive again, but later that week I did. He looked a little thinner and slurred his speech. He could walk only with difficulty. Arabella seemed to have lost both her fangs and her tongue. Solicitous and kind, she wheeled him to the pub where everyone rushed to buy him a drink. The doctors had said he could be helped to make a good recovery. Arabella said that Shaddy and Toby had become their surrogate parents and were keeping them free from want.

'I miss the tango,' Arabella said. 'Sometimes. It makes one visible – a centrepoint. They see. And they see you.' She shook her head like a shaggy wet dog.

In the meantime Lucy avoided me, avoided Judy, Arabella and the park. I suspected that she had gone after Jacobus, to resume her role as his footstool or long-suffering helpmate. But I was not going to let this spoil my life. When the next tea-dance came round, I decided to go.

I was having a good old time waltzing with Beatty Symonson who had a sense of fun similar to Arabella's, always making humorously wicked observations.

'Who is that woman?' she asked. 'She's looking at you as if she could burn a hole through you.'

I turned to look. It was Lucy.

'My one-time fiancée,' I said. 'I hope we're still friends.'

'She's substantial. Too big for floral cover. Tell her to wear plain things – in black, blue or grey. She could be enhanced with contrasting plain colours. No necklaces round that short, thick neck.'

'Where I come from we don't detail people's physical shortcomings. If they are nice, we like them; if they are not, we don't,' I said. 'So don't be a *vache!*'

I introduced Beatty and Lucy. Lucy was her gracious self again. On our own she told me she had hated being partnerless: it was like going without a lump of sugar in her tea. And she did love sugar in her tea. We danced.

'You've changed back to being Lucy, my friend, fiancée and wife-to-be,' I said. 'Are you still willing?'

'I realised I have but one passage through this life and I must live it. I went through hell being jealous of a dead woman.'

'Let's go home. To our garden of delights,' I joked.

'It's probably neglected and overrun with the weeds of desire and frustration.'

I proposed to her again, but this time before we got to bed.

A few weeks later we were married. Not, mind you, with all the fuss and protocol of our first times, but a simple ceremony at our local Registry Office. We were the second couple of the day and with us were Finbar, Judy and Benedicta to shove us off into the murky waters of a second marriage. However much we like to pretend that a second marriage is sailing into clear blue water, there are past adventures, indiscretions and events to colour expectations – and sometimes hidden, jagged rocks.

Lucy was a more than pleasing eyeful in her apricot suit and matching hat. We made our responses confidently. Coyness was for beginners!

With Judy's help, I had arranged for a lunch worthy of the occasion at the ritzy Acres Hotel which, this time round, we could afford.

We strode around the hotel like celebrities, for that was how they treated us. We were joined by other friends including Alana and Jah Garside and Jamsey. I wished Maryanne and Rootsman could have been with us. And we all had a thought for Uncle Nat.

Our lunch was superb and afterwards Finbar insisted on making what he claimed was not a speech.

'It's not a speech,' he protested. 'It's my wisest words. Love is blind… keep it so, and the wrinkles of the years will pass by unnoticed. Go out for a second time, and live faithfully with your chosen someone till the end of the days God has set aside for you. That's all I have to say.'

'Name our day, Finn!' insisted Benedicta. But Finbar joked that he had married her years ago and she had somehow forgotten the event.

'You can't teach an old dog new tricks,' he replied with some tenderness. 'You're an old Stradivarius and you play the sweetest of tunes. So enjoy yourself this fine day as I did on the day I married you.'

'You will be captured and tamed,' she replied. 'You mark my words.' Those two were always nibbling away at each other's sanity, but for me every aspect of the day was satisfying… the style of the table, the food, the intimacy of our friendships and of course the champagne and the wine which had begun to affect Judy. She nodded off once or twice while we waited for coffee. We announced our intention to enjoy a vacation in Jamaica at some future time. As a young man, when I'd married so soon after the war, a honeymoon had been too expensive. But times had changed.

There was much laughter when Jah Garside promised to accompany us and introduce us to what he called 'the theatre of the Kingston streets', to 'jerk pork' and rum in the moonlight and to the compulsion to dance when reggae and ska were played. But that was to be for later. We both felt we had more thinking do do, more adjustments to make in our respective relationships to the Caribbean – which for both of us, for different reasons, was still an uncomfortable past. But we would go there with open hearts and minds.

From now on, Lucy and I were committed to each other, to living in peace and amity till death parted us. Day after day, I would watch the pinkish, reddish skin contrasting with the straps of her brassiere and the marks it imprinted on her shoulder. There was also the fleshy mole that sat like the nipple of a hidden breast on her soft round thigh. I loved that too. She was outgrowing her feelings of inadequacy, was letting go of her hurts and angers. She was beginning to forget that she had never been affirmed or appreciated by the men she loved. Sometimes I felt she worked too desperately to *make* 'happiness', as if happiness was clay and could be moulded to fit. I had learned from my long days alone that the gift of being and feeling happy is something that just comes. It comes when we clear our minds of dross, and love who we can, wherever, whenever we can.

To all who knew the park before the Thatcher years, it had lost its magic. It was open to the gaze; the trees chopped away; the hedges mercilessly shorn and the flowers neglected by the jobbing gardeners (who had put in the lowest tender for the job). They had commandeered our secret places to skive, smoke and gossip in. They busied themselves only when they expected their foreman, otherwise, they did as they liked. The park had been cleansed of trees and beauty. The dogs have become older, slower – more content to sit and dream. Cups of tea in hand, we do the same – but like us the park is dying. Old Thomack, too, has grown older, slower, leaning on his stick and 'breathing with breath' as he says, muttering aloud to the ghosts in his mind. Maryanne writes to him sometimes, and he passes on her messages of love and regard to us. She remains a shadow once thrown by life and time into our park – where the grass grew greener, where flowers bloomed, where roses sneaked their scent into the air and butterflies were so plentiful they were not difficult to discern. We loved the place where words poured out of us like tap water.

What is it like now? A mute and neutered, urban waste-land. A watering hole for the birds that have eyes sharp enough to locate the lily-pond and drop down between flights for a drink. The seats, now repaired, provide some-where for old folks to sit and take the weight off their feet. Some swear they have seen the ghost of Uncle Nat with Barker's ghost at his feet. They have heard him muttering into the wind, 'Blessed are the pure in Heart for they have seen God. In all His complex Glory.'

I dream of a visit to my native Barbados and to Jamaica, when I would certainly do my best to find Rootsman and Maryanne living in peaceful concubinage. Two people who had impressed me so deeply. I believe I would certainly find a moment of happiness then. When we walk in the park I wonder if we will find Jamaica as we dream of it: a magical, ebullient island snuggling in the midst of dancing blue waters. An island of articulate flora and fauna telling of a history that emerges painfully but resiliently through the centuries... I hope so.

In the meantime, above us is the vault of blue adorned with wisps and swathes of clouds, a gift to all of us who looked beyond the phalanx of trees that marked the borders of our park.

Also by Beryl Gilroy

Sunlight on Sweet Water

Beryl Gilroy transports the reader back to the Guyanese village of her childhood to meet such characters as Mr Dewsbury the Dog Doctor, Mama Darlin' the village midwife and Mr Cumberbatch the Chief Mourner.

It was a time when 'children did not have open access to the world of adults and childhood had not yet disappeared'. Perhaps for this reason, the men and women who pass through these stories have a mystery and singularity which are as unforgettable for the reader as they were for the child. Beryl Gilroy brings back to life a whole, rich Afro-Guyanese community, where there were old people who had been the children of slaves and where Africa was not forgotten. *Sunlight on Sweet Water* is fast becoming a Peepal Tree best-seller and is widely taught on women's and Caribbean literature courses.

Price: £6.95
ISBN: 0 948833 64 5

Gather the Faces

Marvella Payne is twenty-seven, works as a secretary for British Rail and has pledged to the congregation of the Church of the Holy Spirit that she will abstain from sex before marriage. When she repulses the groping hands of the trainee-deacon, Carlton Springle, she resigns herself to growing old with her mother, father and Bible-soaked aunts. But Aunt Julie has other ideas and finds Marvella a penfriend from her native Guyana. When good fortune allows the couple to meet, Marvella awakens to new possibilities as she realises how bound she has been by the voices of her dependent, cossetted childhood. But will marriage be another entrapment, another loss of self?

Price £6.99
ISBN 0-948833-88-2

In Praise of Love and Children

After false starts in teaching and social work, Melda Hayley finds her mission in fostering the damaged children of the first generation of black settlers in a deeply racist Britain.

But though Melda finds daily uplift in her work, her inner life starts to come apart. Her brother Arnie has married a white woman and his defection from the family and the distress Melda witnesses in the children she fosters causes her own buried wounds to weep.

Melda confronts the cruelties she has suffered as the "outside child" at the hands of her stepmother. But though the past drives Melda towards breakdown, she finds strengths there too, especially in the memories of the loving, supporting women of the yards. And there is Pa who, in his new material security in the USA, discovers a gentle caring side and teaches his family to sing in praise of love and children.

Price: £6.95
ISBN: 0 948833 89 0

Inkle and Yarico

being the narrative of Thomas Inkle concerning his shipwreck and long sojourn among the Caribs and his marriage to Yarico, a Carib woman.

As a young man of twenty, Thomas Inkle sets out for Barbados to inspect the family sugar estates. On the way he is shipwrecked on a small West Indian island inhabited by Carib Indians. He alone escapes as his shipmates are slaughtered, and is rescued by Yarico, a Carib woman who takes him as, "an ideal, strange and obliging lover." So begins an erotic encounter which has a profound effect on both. Amongst the Caribs, Inkle is a mere child, whose survival depends entirely on Yarico's protection. But when he is rescued and taken with Yarico to the slave island of Barbados, she is entirely at his mercy.

Inkle and Yarico is loosely based on a "true" story which became a much repeated popular narrative in the 17th and 18th centuries. Beryl Gilroy reinterprets its mythic dimensions from both a woman's and a black perspective, but above all she engages the reader in the psychological truths of her characters' experiences.

As an old man, Inkle recalls the Carib's stories as being like 'fresh dreams, newly washed, newly woven and true to the daily lives of the community'. Inkle and Yarico has the same magic and pertinence.

This is a narrative of deep historical insight into the commodifying and abuse of humanity and an excellent book for close study in schools and colleges. Gilroy lays the past bare as a text for the present.

Price: £6.95
ISBN: 0 948833 98 X

About Peepal Tree Press

In the nineteenth century over two million Indians were lured away to work as indentured labourers on the sugar estates of the Caribbean, Mauritius, Fiji and other parts of the Empire. They brought the peepal tree with them and planted in these new environments, a sign of their commitment to their cultural roots.

Peepal Tree focuses on the Caribbean and its Diaspora, and also publishes writing from the South Asian Diaspora and Africa. Its books seek to express the popular resources of transplanted and transforming cultures.

Based in Leeds, Peepal Tree began humbly in a back bedroom in 1986, and has now published over 100 quality literary paperback titles, with fiction, poetry and literary, cultural and historical studies. We publish around 15 English language titles a year, with writers from Guyana, Jamaica, Trinidad, Nigeria, Bangladesh, Montserrat, St Lucia, America, Canada, the UK, Goa, India and Barbados.

Peepal Tree is committed to publishing writing which explores new areas of reality which is multi-ethnic and multicultural. We aim to publish writing of high literary merit which 'makes a difference', which challenges assumptions and leads to cross-cultural understanding. Our list contains work by established authors such as Kamau Brathwaite, Beryl Gilroy, Ismith Khan and David Dabydeen (and lots more!), but we are also strongly committed to publishing new writers.

Feel free to contact us for information about our books and writers and we'll do our best to help. We also offer a full mail order service to anywhere in the world.

Peepal Tree Press, 17, Kings Avenue, Leeds LS6 1QS, United Kingdom
tel +44 (0113) 2451703 e-mail <hannah@peepal.demon.co.uk>
website (from June 2001) http://www.peepaltree.com